RUN, RUN, ROOMMATES

A SPICY OPPOSITES ATTRACT NOVELLA

WINTER WANDERLUST
BOOK 4

LIZ ALDEN

RUN, RUN, ROOMMATES

Copyright © **2025 Liz Alden**

All rights reserved.

ISBN-13 (ebook): 978-1-954705-56-2

ISBN-13 (paperback): 978-1-954705-57-9

Published by **Liz Alden**

This is a work of fiction. Any similarity between the characters and situations within its pages and places or persons, living or dead, is unintentional and coincidental.

First Edition

Library of Congress Control Number: 2025922015

Southampton, Massachusetts, United States of America

Proofread by Dan Janeck

Cover Design by Qamber Designs

ALSO BY LIZ ALDEN

<u>The Love and Wanderlust Series</u>
The Night in Lover's Bay (free prequel short story)
The Fling in Panama
The Slow Burn in Polynesia
The Second Chance in the Mediterranean
The Rival in South Africa (standalone novella)
The Player in New Zealand
The Best Friend in Indonesia (free standalone short story)

<u>Aged Like Fine Wine Series</u>
Rosé with My Fake Fiancé
Riesling with My Roommate
Prosecco with My Professor
Cava with My Colleague

<u>Winter Wanderlust Series</u>
Nutcracker with Benefits
Frosty Proximity
Ghost of Ex-mas Past
Run, Run, Roommates
The Gift of the Matchmaker

<u>Wanderlust Resort Series</u>
Beach Boss (free standalone short story)
Beach Resolution
Put it in Beach Mode

With love and Pride.

TO CONCERNED READERS

This book includes a male main character with homophobic parents (off page) and who has experienced the death of a sibling (past, off page). The female main character experiences cyber sexual harassment (on page).

1

MARCO

There's cinnamon sprinkled on top of the eggnog.

Fuck.

Amid the flurry of decorators and florists and caterers in the penthouse apartment, I dig my phone out of my pocket. I stop next to one of the windows looking out over the Manhattan skyline and text the one person who gets exactly what the cinnamon powder means.

MARCO

There's cinnamon on the eggnog.

BRIN

MOTHER FUCKERS

HOW DARE THEY

Then she sends a text that is nothing but emojis: the frowning devil, the smiling devil, a knife, an evil clown, the skull . . .

I'm lucky she texted back so quickly; she must be on a break at the restaurant. I can picture her in her black server uniform, her wild red hair tamed in a bun but her blue eyes lit up with merriment. She might even be biting her lip to keep back her laughter . . .

Someone nearby giggles, and it echoes the sound of Brin's laughter in my head so much it startles me and I look up.

Two people from the catering team—servers based on their attire, one white with long blonde hair and the other Asian with chin-length black hair—glance at each other like they've got some great secret. And then their gaze returns to me over the massive granite kitchen island.

I raise an eyebrow.

Reading my face, the blonde shrugs. "You have an adorably smitten look on your face. Texting your crush? Partner?"

The other one giggles again.

Smitten? Just because Brin's an extremely attractive woman, one of my closest friends, and one of the kindest, sweetest people I've ever known . . .

I am *not* smitten.

I turn my screen off and pocket my phone, any trace of smittenness . . . smittenity? Smite? No, that's not right. Whatever . . . erased from my face. I pick up the tablet on the counter next to me and tap over to the catering contract, scrolling down until I find paragraph four, item three of the special requests made by my boss. Because I'm his personal assistant, one of my jobs is to make sure everything is executed per his wishes.

On my best days, I'm often told I'm too curt, too practical, too blunt.

Since I arrived at William's place this morning to discover he'd left the balcony doors open last night and there were pigeons (and pigeon shit) everywhere, I've also had to deal with two vendors running late, an event planner that won't answer my calls (not entirely sure I blame her, but still), and now, a very minor problem that's probably not the only one.

It's not one of my best days.

I point at the tray of coupe glasses, the creamy eggnog filled to the brim and topped with stenciled cinnamon creating a variety of patterns across the foam. "Throw those away."

Someone gasps.

"Uhhh . . ." the blonde server says.

The chef, the catering manager, and the event planner are all called over. I point out the special request. Apologies are made and I watch as they remake the next batch, this time sprinkling the tops with cocoa powder.

Now the staff is side-eyeing me. A picky client.

Except it's not actually me who's picky. I'm the messenger. But they'll never know that.

Once the eggnog is decorated correctly, I stalk off to check the rest of the special requests, because apparently you can't trust professionals to do their jobs anymore.

Usually, it's not a problem.

Usually, our regular caterer is available for events, because *usually*, my boss doesn't throw a last-minute holiday party a week before Christmas.

I'm kidding myself, because there is no "usually" with my boss. When he wants the impossible to happen, I'm the one who makes it work, and throwing a last-minute holiday party in his penthouse before he jets off to St. Bart's for Christmas *should be* a cake walk.

I pore through the contract with the event planner, checking the list twice, correcting as much of it as I can before my boss gets here. The evergreen boughs that drape carefully over the fireplace, banister, and railing of the balcony are not the cedar ones we ordered, but fraser, so I send someone out to either get the ones we ordered or more fraser to fill it in better. Two of the servers have no idea which food is free from ginger—William's sister has an allergy, not to mention the assortment of guests on the list who have dairy, gluten, or allium allergies or intolerances, so we have to have a staff meeting to review everything. The caterers have re-plated two trays of appetizers, the bartenders have no rosemary so I have to send someone out *again*, and I'm arguing with the DJ about the lighting arrangement. I'm ready to put my foot so far up his ass, Santa drops coal down his throat to fill my stocking.

That's when, of course, William walks in.

My boss is twenty-seven but tells everyone he's twenty-three. He's got dark hair that falls in waves down to his shoulders, unnaturally high cheekbones, and he's wearing a Givenchy trench coat that is more expensive than my first car over a Stefano Pilati custom-made outfit that when I told Brin how much it cost him, she literally hyperventilated.

I haven't told her about his Labubu collection yet.

William is ridiculously good-looking. When I first learned who he was, my bisexual heart had a moment of pitter-pattering . . . until I met him. I'd never heard of William Robert LeClerc the Third until I was prepping for my interview—and why would I have? William is wildly popular in his own little —albeit, powerful—world of trust fund babies and social climbers.

Not only is he straight, but he's unbearable. Fortunately, I'm getting paid six figures to tolerate him.

Like usual, he walks in gushing over the way we've transformed his penthouse condo. "Divine!" he shouts, walking through the living space. "It smells amazing in here," he crows when he passes through the kitchen. Everyone is full of smiles and *good holiday cheer* by the time William gets to me.

He subtly pinches my elbow. Hard.

"They used the wrong evergreen," he hisses in my ear. Behind his glasses—bold, black frames laced with gold that brings out the matching flecks in his eyes—his gaze is sharp and critical.

"I know. I've been through the—"

"It looks shabby."

"We're getting more," I assure him.

"And the ginger?"

I'm tense and wound up from having to make demands of the staff, but William's concern for his sister softens me.

By about half a percent.

"I went over every recipe with the chef." The catering manager now hates me for putting them behind schedule, stealing their staff for a thorough review of the allergens in each dish, and throwing away several items that were incorrectly prepared, no matter how small the infringement.

"Fine." William somehow manages to shrug me off, even though he's the one that grabbed me.

Blessedly, William retreats to his room after more smiling and over-the-top simpers at the staff for how lovely everything is. I get back to work.

Hours later, the party is finally winding down. I've been running around at William's bidding, bringing him food, reminding him who guests are, and quietly—but firmly—kicking people out who shouldn't be here.

Most of William's guest list don't like me. Possibly because I kicked them out at some other party when they were on the outs with my boss, or possibly because they actually hate my boss and I'm an easier target.

I don't care. I don't get paid to suck up to them.

There are a few lingering guests, but the staff is packing up after William swanned through giving generous tips and superfluous compliments. The staff will remember those tips and those compliments. William comes out on top.

They don't know what I saved them from, because William throwing a hissy fit is a nightmare. Like, *call Daddy's PR team and confiscate people's phones* nightmare.

"Why are you still here?" He peers over his glasses at me,

a move that I'm pleased to say makes him look at least thirty-two, but I won't ever tell him that. He flutters a hand at me. "Go home and don't embarrass me tomorrow."

I have no idea what William is talking about. My mind scrolls through our schedule—William's private flight is at noon. His bags are packed and downstairs with the staff already. The chauffeur will take care of things and then William will be whisked off and I'll get two weeks of vacation.

"Of course," I say, and as soon as William has returned to his guests, I whip out my phone and pore through William's emails, looking for some kind of clue as to what he's referencing.

It takes a few minutes until I find it in his draft folder—along with twenty other messages, mostly empty, which I'll have to deal with at some point—but there it is. An email with the "to" line empty. It's a forwarded chain of emails and I read each one with deepening dread.

Marco,

My dad wants me to take a more active role in our philanthropic efforts so I've signed you up. I don't care how much you do, just do enough to make Dad happy.

WRLIII

Yes, his email signature includes his suffix to be sure you don't get him confused with his father or his ninety-two-year-old grandfather.

There's an attachment, and a thread of emails from a charity organization confirming "my" registration. I click on a link, which opens to a lush green website with gilded filigree, golden snowflakes, and shiny ribbons. The only text is a hotel name—one of the chains in Manhattan—and in big block text, a countdown.

SIX HOURS TO THE START OF THE SHiNY SEASON!

What the fuck is *SHiNY*?

I do a quick internet search. SHiNY stands for Scavenger Hunt in New York, and based on their flagship event, which takes place in the summer, it's a multiday scavenger hunt to raise money for charity. The summer event is an over-the-top celebration of the city, with multiple articles written about the good it does for the various organizations it raises money for.

William having me fill in for him at a charity event like this is fine, it's part of my job—although having to do this over the time I thought was going to be my vacation time is an absolute pain in my ass. But what I realize with a sinking sense of dread is that SHiNY Season is set up to celebrate the holidays in the same over-the-top way.

And I fucking hate this time of year.

2

BRIN

ARANCINI IS THE WORST.

The little round fried balls of cheese and rice are amazingly delicious and when there's any leftovers in the kitchen after the restaurant closes, they're the first to get snapped up and taken home.

Here's the thing, though. These little balls are tumbleweeds from hell.

They're crispy and crunchy on the outside, and when you pair that with the rimless modern dinnerware we use in the restaurant, it's a recipe for disaster.

The service staff all know it. But our chef, Helena, refuses to remedy the situation by, I don't know, adding a bed of *marinara sauce* to the plate. Even a bed of lettuce would work. Even me, Brin Shaw, a backwoods nobody from Appalachia, knows how to fix this problem.

Although I suppose that if the arancini had been on a bed of marinara sauce, it's possible that I would have accidentally dropped a marinara-coated arancini into this lady's purse, which would have made the situation about a thousand times worse.

Eva, my best friend here at the restaurant, and I watched it happen in slow motion. I had just picked up the plate from the tray of appetizers and was moving to set it down in the middle of the table. Someone had stood up from their seat right in my path. I dodged. A collision was avoided.

But I heard that little plop as the arancini rolled off the plate and into the bag.

"What do we do?" I hiss at Eva as I return to her and we both pick up plates.

We're conferring over the tray of appetizers every time we grab a dish, trying to hide our conversation over the din of the diners and "Santa Baby" playing on the restaurant's speakers.

She picks up the calamari. I pick up the stuffed mushrooms.

"You have to dig it out," she says.

Two plates of bruschetta.

"If I get caught they'll think I'm stealing her wallet."

A flatbread and another calamari.

"So don't get caught."

By the time we put all the appetizers out, I'm no closer to a plan. I mournfully look at the purse. Why does she have to be sitting with her back to the entire restaurant? Even if I could distract her, the tables nearby would totally see me.

When we get back to the server station, I turn pleading eyes to Eva. "We can do this together. I'll provide cover, you get the ball out of her purse."

"I think you need to leave it."

I press my hands together. "Please. I cannot live with myself if I leave it. I'll be sleepless tonight, worrying that she'll call in and report it and then I'll get fired. You know I cannot lose this job."

Eva sighs. "If you would sign up for Sugary again, you wouldn't be so strapped."

"I know," I admit. I haven't told Eva the real reason why I

don't want to get back onto the so-called dating app. "This is my Christmas wish to you."

That gets a smile out of her. "I thought your Christmas wish was to lose your 'virginity'?" She even does the air quotes. Eva is the only person in my life who knows that pesky little fact about me, and she's made it clear that having p-in-v sex is a bigger milestone in my head than it is in real life.

I waggle a finger at her. "That one I do not want your help with."

"Fine," she says, and then she holds the large tray out to me. "But you didn't deny it. We'll circle back to that later. For now, you hold this. Block the view the best you can."

"Got it."

I dutifully follow her out to the table. Eva pulls me close to her, the tray clutched to my other side, and beelines right for the woman.

Quick as a cat when we get there, Eva bends down and snatches up the purse. I'm too busy blocking the view to see if she is able to retrieve the arancini.

"Miss," she says. "Your purse fell off the back here." Eva puts the purse right back where she found it.

"Oh. Thank you."

Eva smiles and makes a show of checking on the rest of the table. We retreat back to the station and Eva holds out her hand. Inside is a mushed rice ball.

Thank you baby Jesus in a manger.

THE REST OF THE NIGHT PASSES IN A WHIRLWIND. THE HOLIDAYS are *bananas*. Even on a Thursday night at midnight, our restaurant is still bustling. I've already been tipped hundreds of dollars, and our largest party—the one with the arancini purse lady—hasn't even left yet.

Now, though, the kitchen is closing up and our manager, Alice, is subtly telling the rowdy group of dentists—and assistants and office staff—that they have to move on.

Eva is counting her cash and checking her receipts so she can close up and leave. I offered to finish with the big table so she can meet her date from Sugary.

The thought makes my stomach dip in an uncomfortable way. But Eva assures me this guy is legit—hasn't even tried to sleep with her yet.

In fact, she proudly showed off the manicure he paid for before their last date. Next week he's taking her to some charity event. Tonight they're meeting for drinks, and she has a change of clothes in her locker.

"Where is he taking you tonight?" I ask.

"Nix's," she says. "Wanna come? You could meet us when you get off and I bet my date would pay for your drinks."

I haven't even heard of it and assuming some guy would pay for my drinks feels cringy. I only moved to the city about two years ago, and I don't have the spare money to go out to the kinds of places Eva's dates take her. Not when every dollar I earn goes to paying off my debt instead of outrageously expensive cocktails since I don't have a sugar daddy.

"No thanks," I say quickly. "But I hope you have a great time."

She sighs, pretending to be put out to tease me. "At least you're coming to my Christmas party."

"Yeah, sorry Marco's not going to come."

"The grinch who hates Christmas probably isn't the best person to have at a Christmas party anyway." Eva's smile softens it. She likes my roommate, just not this side of him.

"Stop it," I chide. "His brother died around the holidays. He never mentions his parents, he's not religious. There are plenty of aspects of Christmas not to like."

Last year, when we were fairly new roommates, I'd tried to innocently ask Marco what he wanted for Christmas. I was going to get him a gift, but I wasn't sure what, because what do you get the guy who has everything?

He'd looked me dead in the eye and said he doesn't celebrate because last time he'd had a Christmas tree, his brother was hit by a car carrying it home.

Eva winces. "That's terrible. But *you* love Christmas," Eva says. "And so do I. We'll just have to enjoy the season without Marco."

I head back to the table with a tray of drinks—hot toddies, mint martinis, and for someone less in the holiday spirit, whiskey on the rocks. When I get back, Eva's talking to someone at the bar, and my stupid little heart lights up in happiness at the sight of my roommate.

I walk behind the bar to hear her telling the story of the wayward arancini to him. Of course, she tells it better than I would, making the story hilarious and pantomiming her quick fingers.

Marco's smiling at her across the bar, and I get a pang of jealousy in my chest. They're both New Yorkers, and sometimes it feels like they bond over my quaint, Appalachian mannerisms.

This stupid crush on him has got to stop.

I take a minute to grab a clean glass and the soda gun, filling it with Diet Coke. I slide it over to him as Eva wraps up the story. Marco smiles at me, and I take him in—fitted suit still immaculate, but tired eyes and rumpled hair.

"That's how I saved Brin's job today," she finishes. She smiles at me, teasingly, and I bump her hip with mine.

Eva did save my bacon. Just like Marco, who has given me a safe space to live. Where would I be without these two saving me from all my stupid decisions?

Eva's my best friend. She's been here a lot longer than I have—she trained me when I started. She also has a friend group that she organizes to get together for brunch once a week at another restaurant owned by the same management company, which means we get an employee discount.

Most of the friends we go out with are Eva's friends from school. I'm getting to know them, but since I see Eva almost every day, we're much closer.

"You should get out of here; you've got your hot date," I tell her.

"True." She squeezes me goodbye and waves to Marco before sauntering off.

I tilt my head at him. "What are you doing here?"

"Walking you home."

Marco does this occasionally, when he's out as late as I'm working. I look down to hide my smile. In the bar sink there's a few dirty glasses, so I grab them and run them through the sudsy water and the brush.

"I still have a table." I jut my chin at the twenty-top on the far side of the restaurant.

"I'll wait."

Fifteen minutes later the group finally wraps up, and they leave behind a generous tip. I hand most of it over to my manager for the tip pool, since the back-of-house staff deserve a cut and then the rest goes to Eva. I run through closing, and Marco and I are some of the last people to leave.

It's chilly out, but I'm still warm from hustling around the restaurant, so I keep my coat open for now, and when Marco and I turn left on the sidewalk I tip my chin up and puff out a breath of cold air like a dragon.

"I have an ulterior motive," he starts.

"What?" I gasp in mock horror. "You didn't come to walk me home just because you're a nice guy?"

He gives me side-eye. "I'm not a nice guy."

"Of course you are," I argue back. Marco is nice . . . to me. "Besides, you know what all the bad guys say, right?" I swerve to bump him. "They call themselves nice guys. It's like the bad guy pledge." I hold up one hand like I'm being sworn in. "I, Chad E. Villain—the E stands for evil, by the way—do solemnly swear that I'm a nice guy."

I joke, but there's a lot of truth behind the humor. The worst of the men smile at you, play nice, until you see the horns hidden in their perfectly combed hair.

Speaking of *actually* nice guys, Marco slings his arm around my shoulder. My heart goes pitter-patter because he's so warm and solid and he tugs me close enough to feel the press of his body—

That's when I hear footsteps coming from behind us. Fast footsteps.

I grip my purse harder and Marco's arm tightens around my shoulders. It's late, and even though the streets of New York are lit up with all the stoplights and bar signs, there's not as many people walking around as I'd like. A yawning opens in my stomach.

All that takes a split second to register, and then we're being passed by a person running. They're not wearing normal workout gear, so I doubt they're jogging for the exercise.

Marco and I relax slightly. His arm still stays around me though, so I lean into him more.

What would I have done if that person had bad intentions? What if Marco wasn't walking me home? He's so protective of me—so much that I worry he thinks of me as a little sister. I can't blame him, and he doesn't even know the half of it.

But still, it stings. Marco is so attractive, so put together. Even now, with his tired eyes and slightly crumpled suit, he's got an aura of control around him.

No one would *dare* try to pull one on Marco.

We're quiet for a few calming heartbeats, and then I remember what Marco was saying. "So why *are* you here, if not to keep me company and protect me from rando bad guys?"

I peer up at him as he runs his free hand through his hair. Marco has great hair: dark, wavy, a little long.

He's also a foot taller than me. From this angle I can also see his Adam's apple, which I am mildly obsessed with.

It has no right to be so sexy. It's practically obscene. Which makes me feel . . . complicated. Good Catholic girls don't pine for their roommate.

Although I do a lot of things since I've moved to the city that good Catholic girls wouldn't do—I just do them with a hefty side of guilt.

"I need your help."

I'm jolted back to the real world, where Marco's my roommate and not someone I can randomly lick.

"I'm assuming this is work related."

He nods.

"What did Billy Bob do now?" I tease. His boss's nickname gets a barely-there smile from Marco. "Of course, I'm in." It's the least I can do, since Marco has done so much for me. When we met one night at a bar, I was at my wit's end, drowning in debt and realizing that I was scared to go home. I was desperate, and it could have turned out so poorly, could have been another stupid decision I made because I couldn't take care of myself.

Instead it was the best thing I ever did—aside from leaving Tennessee. Thanks to Marco, my rent is cheap and my apartment is luxurious—for my budget, anyway—so I'll do whatever I can for him.

He grimaces. "You may want to wait until you hear what you're committing to."

I grin at him. "It can't be that bad. Hit me."

He looks down at me, his Adam's apple disappearing from view, so instead I focus on his dark eyes. "It's something called SHiNY. All I know is that it's a holiday-themed scavenger hunt for charity."

"A fundraiser?" I echo. "That doesn't sound too bad." It

sounds right up my alley. I love any excuse to celebrate Christmas, even though I'm not religious anymore.

"A days-long event, culminating on the twenty-third, where we have to spend our time running all over the city completing tasks and making fools of ourselves. The teams can be two people, and there's no way I can do this myself. That's why I need your help."

"Of course you would hate that." I laugh. "I'm already a fool, so I'm halfway there. What are the tasks?"

He shakes his head. "We don't know yet. But we have to show up at the opening event at four p.m. tomorrow. It might be . . . it might be a lot." Marco looks at me apologetically.

"Holiday-themed? For charity?" *And spending time every day with Marco*, I don't add out loud. "Say less, I'm in."

3

MARCO

Brin and I arrive home to our two-bedroom apartment that we share with another woman, Bea.

About fourteen months ago, back when I'd been a regular at a bar down the street from William's penthouse, I was downing whiskey neat, trying to forget the way I'd yelled at William's nutritionist. It had been a glass-shattering moment, realizing that I was William's attack dog, the fixer, the one who got their hands dirty so William could be the nice one.

My brother was right. I was an asshole.

Next to me, a woman had hoisted herself onto the empty barstool. She ordered a shot of bottom-shelf tequila and tossed it back, grimacing as it burned going down.

I winced in sympathy. Then she ordered another.

"Make it a Cutwater. I'll take one too," I said to the bartender. "On me," I told the redhead when she looked at me, eyes wide. "I've had a shitty day, and a shot sounds perfect."

"Yeah?" she huffed at me. "Did you just get fired? Did one of your roommates skip town without telling you, leaving you with two months of rent to pay and one last roommate who always has a creepy boyfriend hanging around?"

Her face had twisted into a fierce scowl, which was at odds with her accent. *Tellin' you.*

"Shit," I said.

We talked, and it became clear to me that she was a sweet young woman who didn't know how to defend herself against jaded and overly practical New Yorkers. Just like my brother.

We switched to drinks instead of shots. She confessed that it was her name only on the lease, and her remaining roommate (and her creepy boyfriend) had refused to chip in to cover rent.

Oh you sweet summer child.

In a hushed whisper, she'd told me that a few months ago, she hadn't washed her roommate's dishes for four days, and she'd seen a rat in the kitchen before work that day. And a few weeks ago, the knob had mysteriously disappeared from the bathroom door.

She'd told me she'd been sleeping on a futon in the living room with a curtain for privacy. And she couldn't afford better.

"You'd be better off sharing a room; at least you'd have a door," I told her.

"Anything would be better than a place I can't afford."

At this point, I was tipsy, and this conversation had too many echoes of ones I'd had with my brother. I wasn't going to be happy knowing Brin was out there without help. I wish someone had been there to look after my brother when he'd first come to the city.

"You should come stay with me until you find some place better," I threw out.

Brin looked at me, her eyes bright. I probably shouldn't be proposing this while we'd been drinking, but Brin was still working on the gin and tonic she'd ordered after those two shots . . . which, once I thought about it, had been two hours ago. I explained to her that my roommate had a new partner and he wasn't around much. One late-night call and I'd gotten permission to let Brin stay in his bedroom.

"Wouldn't it be weird to share an apartment with a woman?" she asked.

"Why?"

She thought about it. "I guess because there's a potential for sex?"

A sizzle went through me, but I tamped it down. Brin did not need that, and I wouldn't be yet another person to take advantage of her. "Well, if it makes you feel any better, I'm bi, so any roommate I have could, hypothetically, be my type."

"Oh," she said. Was me being queer a deal breaker? She swallowed the last of her drink. "Okay, but I'm not a charity case. I'll stay a week, tops."

"How about if you haven't found a place within a week, you start paying me rent?" That way she would be safe.

"Deal." We shook on it. After we left the bar, we housed dollar pizza slices to soak up the booze, and I walked her home, helped her pack what we could carry, and moved her in, giving her my bed while I slept on the couch. The next day, Greg and I brought her futon back to my place while she was at work.

The same futon she sleeps on now in our room.

I definitely didn't think that I would end up sharing a room with her, but when Brin started paying me rent, it was obvious she couldn't afford much. And then the lease was up, and when my former roommate officially moved in with his partner, we started looking for a new place. We wasted a lot of time trying to find an apartment we could afford on Brin's budget that wasn't awful, and we were both getting discouraged.

I knew Bea from a networking event, and when she said she was looking for a roommate, I jumped on it even though it was a two-bedroom, suggesting that Brin share a room with me. I knew I could trust Bea as a roommate and it was a really safe, nice building.

It meant she had a safe place to stay with someone she trusted, and we worked out a rent that was cheap enough for her to afford without feeling like I was treating her like a charity case.

Now, Brin is my best friend. And when I'd seen that the SHiNY teams are made up of two people, I immediately thought of her.

This is just the type of thing she would love. I've lost track of the number of times we've had to stop to look at a window display or the times I've caught her gawking at the Rocke-feller Center Christmas tree. Last year, I could tell she wasn't excited to go home for the holidays, and she isn't even both-ering to fly home this year.

Maybe this event is exactly what Brin needs.

Bea's already asleep in her room, so Brin and I carefully tiptoe around our nighttime routines. We don't do this often, having different work schedules, but I love moving around the room we share together.

Our room has a queen-sized bed on one side (mine) and a futon on the other (Brin's). Her side of the bedroom has been lightly decorated for Christmas. Last year, Brin went to her parent's for the holidays, so I had the whole place to myself.

I did not decorate, and neither did anyone else. What would have been the point? They were gone, and I sure as hell wasn't going to celebrate the shittiest time of year.

This year, though, Brin is home. I've just come from William's extravagant holiday party, one where the garland was real and the decor was expensive and color-coordinated. William had gone with a pearl-and-gold theme, and every-thing had glimmered and shone.

Here, Brin's decorated on a budget that was probably one percent of William's decor expenses, if that. Next to her bed is a fat red candle circled by fake garland, the leaves of which have been rubbed bare on one side, which Brin tactfully turned away from the door so only she can see it. In a nod to her Catholic upbringing, there's a nativity scene on the corner of her dresser. Instead of camels, though, she's got cheap plastic goats, her favorite animal. Around the window, snowflake lights twinkle in blue.

She gets the shower first, so I gather my clothes for tonight and set aside an outfit for my run first thing in the morning. I won't set an alarm, since William is out of town, but I doubt I'll be able to sleep much past my normal time. I mix my overnight oats, and then, with nothing else to do, sit on my bed, scrolling my phone and trying to think about other things than a naked Brin on the other side of the wall.

One reason Brin and I are able to share a bedroom so well is that she's always working. Sixty hours at the restaurant most weeks, plus a few odd jobs dog walking for the neighbors or babysitting for the single mom two floors up.

I don't know where all the money goes. Brin lives an austere life.

I would give anything to be able to slip Brin a hundred dollars and tell her she could only use it for something fun, but she already worries about being a charity case.

The bedroom door opens and Brin shuffles in, yawning. She's wearing candy cane pajama pants that trail on the floor at her feet and a black tank top—no bra. Both her nipples point through the ribbed fabric and I avert my eyes. Her red hair is up in the microfiber turban that she often leaves hooked on the arm of the futon, the one she's replaced the elastic on about a dozen times.

My eyes are drawn back to her when she gasps. "Look! The lights are working again!" Brin grew up in rural Tennessee, so she drawls everything, especially when she's excited. *Working* is *workin'* and *again* sounds like *agin*. Brin kneels on her futon, which she keeps in couch mode. She claims it's cozier to sleep on it like this, but I think she doesn't want to take up too much space in our room. She inspects the colored light strands that twine through the futon frame.

There are three strands, and a couple days ago one of them went out. They were basic multicolored lights, none of them matching perfectly.

Hopefully she doesn't notice that the strand that was out this morning is slightly more symmetrically wound around the frame than the other two, or that the wire is black instead of green.

My chest goes warm just looking at her. Most people might think I don't get the "true meaning of Christmas" because I don't celebrate and hate the holiday. But that's not true. I do get the true meaning of Christmas.

It's not the hypocrisy of so many Christians that casts out their vulnerable people while simultaneously preaching about a child born in a manger out of necessity.

It's not about people like my boss, who take lavish vacations and seek validation from others by throwing expensive, exclusive parties.

What it is about is the joy that Brin gets on her face, the simple pleasures of having a space that's your own, and a warmth in your heart.

After all the loss in my life I never expected to feel that again. But as Brin hums a melody—"Happy Xmas (War is Over)," by John Lennon, I think—I snatch up my clothes and go to take my shower.

A cold shower.

Because my thoughts have wandered to what it would be like to kiss her, to pull off that tank top and give her so much pleasure she can't stand it. But the last thing Brin needs is someone making her uncomfortable in her own home.

Again.

4

BRIN

WHEN I WAKE UP IN THE MORNING, MARCO'S BED IS EMPTY AND his stack of running clothes is gone.

I get out of bed and light the candle on my nightstand, a thick red one that I've started lighting every day since the day after Thanksgiving that's scented with "Holiday Sparkle." Whatever that is, I like it. This one's much better quality than the one I got last year, because the candle last year melted down to the metal the week before Christmas. This one is still halfway intact, so it's definitely going to make it all the way to the twenty-fifth.

Bea's door is cracked open, but it's the last Friday before her Christmas vacation starts, so I know she's at work, and the apartment has that supernaturally still feeling of an empty space. I have the place to myself right now.

There's a cup of coffee waiting for me at the machine—thanks to Marco—which I gratefully gulp down since it's lukewarm, and then make another cup.

Today I'm babysitting for Andrea, who lives upstairs. Her kid, Noah, is eight, and on Christmas break. Andrea's a sanitation worker, and her mom is a nurse, and they need someone to fill in the gaps between their two schedules.

They pay a reasonable wage and the kid is fun—I know way more about Roblox than I ever desired to. But it makes me feel like a teenager, so desperate for money that I'll take whatever job I can get. Most people my age are hiring babysitters, not working as one.

I mainline caffeine while I watch a few videos to figure out what's new in the world of gaming so I can keep up a conversation with Noah. After babysitting, I'll be working at the restaurant again tonight.

It's a tough schedule, and a long day. But I like helping Andrea out and the tips at the restaurant are great over the holidays. Actually, pretty much since the start of December I've been taking home way more money than I ever have before.

And as much as possible goes to paying off my credit card debt.

It's embarrassingly large. I had no idea what I was doing when I moved to New York City at twenty-three. I didn't know how to be an adult—and two years later, I still don't know how to be one. Most of the time I feel more like three raccoons in a trench coat than a functioning adult.

I don't know how I got to be so lucky to meet and move in with Marco. And even Bea, who is kind, though so busy I rarely see her.

They both have their shit together better than I can even dream.

For example, if I was a fiscally responsible adult, I could have decorated the apartment for the holidays. I could afford a big, beautiful, real tree and the lights to go on it instead of the crappy strands that may or may not light up every time I flick them on.

There's no point in doing any of that, though. Bea is leaving for Christmas, spending the week in upstate New York with her family.

And Marco . . . well. Marco hates Christmas, which I can

understand. It's hard to celebrate a holiday when it reminds you of your brother's death.

So it's not worth it to decorate the apartment just for me. Not when I could be saving that money.

At least I have this scavenger hunt to look forward to.

And with that thought, I hop into the shower.

Living in such close quarters with a man is weird, but we make it work. Marco has a shelf of toiletries in the shower. I open his body wash and take a big sniff. I can tell it's expensive just from its bottle, a simple black-and-white typography-heavy design.

It smells Christmassy. I check the label. Cedar and saffron. I guess it's the cedar that I smell most.

Marco always smells good. I wouldn't have said cedar, but more like a scent that's just . . . him.

It's most noticeable after his runs. Since mornings are when we are most likely to be home together, I usually see Marco when he gets home from running. He runs almost every day, often to a gym to lift weights and then back home, two workouts in one.

It took me about eight weeks after moving in with him to get my libido to calm down. Living with a really hot, pragmatic guy had taken some getting used to. I seriously had thought something was wrong with me, because I'd never had so many "sinful thoughts." I wanted to hand him my life and let him tell me how to be an adult, while at the same time not wanting him to know how out of control things were. Men who have their shit together—and are kinda bossy about it—are my kink, apparently.

(Two years ago I would never have even wanted to *think* of the word kink. I mentally congratulate myself while I lather up my body wash.)

My attraction to Marco means I keep my vibrator well-hidden and take advantage of any alone time I have in the apartment.

And then my libido hit rock bottom after that disaster of a date from Sugary, and now I just don't date. Period.

I wouldn't even have a vibrator if it weren't for Eva. She's gifted me several in the time I've known her, which is the only reason I have one. *Good girls do not have vibrators* is the thought I have to push away every time I look at it.

But right now, I reach up onto my tippy toes and grab the removable showerhead. It's definitely the best feature of this place. I'd never had one before, so the discovery that it worked even better than my vibrator was a pleasant surprise.

I put a foot up on the ledge of the tub and lean against the wall. Depending on where I am with my cycle, I either like the high-pressure setting or the pulse one. Today feels like a pulse one, and I aim the showerhead between my legs and close my eyes.

Dark brooding eyes and a tall runner's build wait for me in my imagination.

5

MARCO

I TAKE THE STAIRS TWO AT A TIME UP TO OUR APARTMENT. BEA'S at work, since this is the Friday before Christmas, but she's leaving tonight.

Brin's home though, and when I walk through the apartment, the shower is running. Last night we'd talked about her schedule and she's babysitting this afternoon and working at the restaurant every night up to the twenty-third. Not ideal for the scavenger hunt, but since we have no idea what the tasks are and I have my days free, we'll do the best we can.

I stand in the kitchen, chugging water and cooling off. I sprinted home, so I'm breathing hard and pacing the apartment when I hear a moan through the wall.

Skidding to a stop, I listen. Was that like an *oh this hot water feels so good* moan, or was it—

I swallow thickly when she moans again. That was definitely a pending-orgasm moan.

Jesus.

In all our time living together, I've never heard her like this. My imagination is running wild right now.

Usually, I'm already running errands for William at this time or in morning meetings. Brin has the apartment to herself most days. But on this rare day off that I have, our schedule has collided in a way that's going to fry my brain.

I'm hard and aching because it's been at least a year since I've been with anyone—my last relationship was with a woman I'd met at one of William's events and we were fuck buddies for a few months—and right now I have my extremely hot roommate pleasuring herself with one measly door between us.

Brin's a great roommate. Neat and tidy, but that doesn't mean I haven't seen her dirty laundry, hang-drying lace underwear, or the vibrator she keeps in her nightstand.

FML.

I cannot make things weird for her. Any attraction I have has to be tamped down, because it's never going to happen. The rent Brin pays me is way below market rate for a nice place like this, and I would never forgive myself if she felt like she moved out because I made her uncomfortable.

I force myself to focus on some of my finest moments as William's personal assistant. Threatening litigation to an ungodly number of people. Giving an adorable puppy to a shelter because he peed on a painting William left on the floor. Getting numerous people fired.

Being William's evil lackey is my superpower, and boy is it a boner-killer.

At least, until Brin's moans get louder and come to a high-pitched crescendo before a guttural ending.

Fuck.

Sweet, naive Brin just had an orgasm in our shower. The water turns off and I realize I need to not be standing in the living room like an idiot when she opens the door. I need a few minutes to get myself under control so I can pretend like everything's normal. I escape out onto the streets and sprint a few more laps around the block.

———

WHEN I GET BACK FROM MY SECOND RUN, BRIN HAS LEFT TO babysit so I have the place to myself. I shower, unable to resist jerking off in the same space Brin had just climaxed in, trying not to think of running my fingers through red hair and kissing freckles.

It doesn't work.

After that, I put on a TV show and answer emails for William, even though I'm technically on vacation. Brin should be down any minute now so we can go to the hotel for the start of SHiNY, so I get dressed.

And wait.

And wait.

Finally Brin comes careening in. "Sorry, Andrea's mother was running late to get home from the hospital."

We rush out the door to make it in time to the ballroom. There's plenty of people milling around already. I wonder how many teams will be participating in the scavenger hunt —there are seats for at least a hundred people. The room is draped with red and gold, potted evergreens lining the walls, light sparkling off the baubles dangling from their branches. Christmas music plays over the speakers, an upbeat "Deck the Halls" barely audible over the hum of voices.

It's enough holiday cheer to make me roll my eyes. Is the whole event going to be like this? So much for ignoring Christmas this year.

Ever since Brin and I moved in together, I've had to shove my attraction to her away. The last thing she needs is to be taken advantage of by anyone else—she's had enough of that with past roommates and former bosses. I know what a great deal I offered her when she moved in with me, and now that I know her better, I see how hard she works.

She reminds me of my brother. Too kind.

Like now, she tugs on my sleeve. "This is outrageous." Her eyes are wide as she takes in the decorations and the attire in the room. "How is this event making any money?

Who's paying for these decorations? I have so many questions."

"I don't know. But rich people like to have money lavished on them first; they can't just write a check and save everyone the trouble," I mutter. I've seen William be courted for his money plenty.

"Marco!" A familiar voice shouts my name from my right and I look over. My friend Greg is shuffling down the row as people make way for him, moving their knees to the side or outright standing up. "Excuse me, excuse me, thanks, yeah, excuse me." Finally Greg plops down next to Brin and gives me a grin. "Hey man."

We shake hands over Brin, who leans back to give us space. Greg is another personal assistant; his boss, Ishimoto Hikaru, is an artist who runs vaguely in the same social circles as William. There is one of Ishimoto's works in William's house right now, actually, and several more in storage. When our schedule allows, Greg and I get together to run or play basketball, though it doesn't happen often.

"Ishimoto has you busy over the holidays too, huh?" I raise my chin to the stage, where it looks like things are about to get started.

Greg straightens his suit jacket. "You know it. All for a good cause, right?" Greg's a good-looking guy—straight, unfortunately for me—and the life of the party. The few times we've gone out together we've ended our nights late and each of us found someone to take home for the night.

It's been a while, though. Not since I moved in with Brin, I guess. If I'm out that late, I swing by Brin's bar and hang out while she closes and then we walk home together. Greg always gives me shit for ditching him, but I like knowing Brin gets home safe.

And having a roommate—an *actual* roommate sharing one room—doesn't give me a lot of privacy. There's a difference between jerking off in the shower when Brin's not home and bringing a random hookup to our shared bedroom.

Now, though, Greg turns to Brin and gives her a dazzling smile, holding out a hand and introducing himself. Then he introduces us to his teammate, Luis, a younger guy with light brown skin, also wearing a suit. Luis works at one of the art galleries in Chinatown. I'm sure I've been there before but can't remember meeting him.

Brin mumbles her name and sinks back down into her chair. Giving us room to talk in front of her, I guess, but Greg studies her for a moment. "Have we met?" he asks.

"I don't think so," Brin says quickly, eyes on her coffee. I can't catch her eye because she tilts the cup to down the last gulp and then the music fades and even though I stare at her face for a moment, Brin doesn't look at me. She looks straight ahead as the presentation starts.

A Black woman is at the podium, holding her hands up for quiet. When the voices hush, she smiles.

"Welcome to SHiNY Season!"

There's a round of applause, with Brin clapping enthusiastically next to me. Everyone is excited for the next few days, but I'm dreading it. I've been able to avoid the worst of holiday cheer for the past few years, but this time, I'm going to be drowning in it.

All this scavenger hunt is going to do is remind me of the worst two Christmases of my life.

6

BRIN

LISTENING TO THIS WOMAN REVVING US UP FULL OF HOLIDAY cheer with a booming voice and an exuberant slideshow should be exactly my jam, but Greg at my side feels like I'm being haunted with the ghost of a bad date.

Greg, the man that I met last year on Sugary.

As the woman up front is talking about the organizations that will benefit from the event, I tug at the hat on my head—a warm and slouchy knit cap that covers my hair. That's probably why he doesn't recognize me—my red hair would be a dead giveaway.

"SHiNY Season is Scavenger Hunt in New York's newest event to celebrate the most generous time of year."

I shift closer to Marco. I had no idea that he knew Greg, but I shouldn't be surprised. They're cut from the same cloth. Handsome white guys, more comfortable in suits, eager to please their bosses, cutthroat when they have to be.

Marco denies being a nice guy. Greg only *thinks* he's a nice guy.

And now I've got Greg sitting right next to me, a friend of Marco's, who's got my whole body on edge, and not in a good way. I hate the shame that runs through me. I still can't believe I signed up for a sugar daddy app, but I bet Greg didn't even think twice about it.

"SHiNY already has an annual event, RUSH NY, which will be in its seventh year next summer," the woman on stage says. It draws my attention back to her, and just in time. "Just like RUSH, SHiNY Season will benefit nine charitable organizations chosen by the board. This year's recipients are . . ."

She runs through the list, taking a moment to talk about each organization. It's a variety—from an animal shelter to a community farm. I'm impressed, actually. I was a smidge worried that we'd be supporting some nonsense organization for a tax write-off for the wealthy, but I've heard of a few of these charities.

When she's done, she turns to logistics. "Each team will get access to the Discord server in a few minutes. There are two types of challenges: open challenges, which you'll be given a list of today and can be completed anytime; and burst challenges, which are open to all participating teams for a limited time."

She clicks to the next screen, which displays a points rubric.

"This is how you'll be scored. Every task description will include how many points you will collect from completing it. At the end, points will be awarded to each team for creativity. Those points will be decided by our panel of judges and awarded on December twenty-seventh, followed by the final tally. Creativity counts for forty percent of your points, so don't be in such a rush to complete a task that you forget to do it with flair."

Next to me, Marco shifts and leans into me. "Holiday flair, huh? That makes you my secret weapon."

Greg's head turns, listening and watching Marco and me.

I smile, but it feels wobbly and of course Marco notices, doing a double take, his brows drawing together in confusion, or maybe concern.

Mentally shaking myself, I try again, and this smile feels better. Marco's frown eases a bit, and he turns back to the presenter.

"We are so thrilled this year to announce that we have some of the highest pledges on record. Pledges are per point awarded to the team, so the more tasks you accomplish, with as much flair as possible, the more you'll raise for charity. If you're familiar with the other scavenger hunts that SHiNY has run in the past, you'll know that no team will score a perfect hundred points. The team with the most points, however, will receive a position of honor at the celebration party, a bundle of gifts donated by our generous sponsors, and the ability to direct ten percent of the funds raised to an organization of their choosing."

There are murmurs of excitement all around the room. Marco and Greg raise eyebrows at each other over my head.

The woman smiles out at the crowd. "I'm glad you're as excited as we are. But if I can have your attention for one last minute, I'll let you go to start the game. Your first task is waiting for you at the back door as you leave: a box of toys, with all the supplies necessary to wrap and deliver the gifts to Toys for Tots. And now . . ." She clicks to the next slide, and a QR code fills the screen. "Let the games begin."

Marco insists on paying for a ride home, which is fine with me. The box full of toys and supplies isn't heavy but it's bulky and cumbersome. After Marco and I scanned the QR code and joined the Discord server, we had shuffled slowly out of the hall behind everyone else waiting to get their box of toys. I had to spend most of that time staring at the back of Greg's head . . . er, his shoulders, because he's taller than me.

Okay, it was his shoulder blades. Fine, whatever, I'm short. Most of the time I hate it, because men already feel intimidating as it is. It's a rare man whose height makes me feel safe.

Like Marco behind me right now, a reassuring hand on the small of my back as we wade through the crowd. We get separated from Greg and don't see him again, thank god. I don't want to give him a chance to recognize me, to bring up how we've met before.

Back at our apartment, I immediately begin unpacking the box, while Marco brings his laptop out of our room and sits on the couch, his long legs stretching out in front of him.

"What are you doing?" I ask.

"Creating a strategy. What are you doing?"

I throw my hands out and survey the mess around me. I've already un-shrink-wrapped one of the rolls of wrapping paper—a shiny vaguely wintery silver—and stacked the toys according to size. "Earning us points. I only have half an hour before I need to leave for work."

Marco leans forward. "Is your plan to just do every task as they're presented to you?"

"How else would you do it? And this is the only task we have so far."

Marco sighs and rolls his eyes, but it's in an exasperated how-silly-are-you way. He leans back and pats the couch cushion next to him. "Come here."

I roll forward over my crossed legs and crawl toward the couch. Marco's dark eyes meet mine for the briefest of seconds before his jaw tightens and he looks away.

I hide a snort. He's so annoyed that I'm diving right in instead of making a plan.

When I plop down next to him, I peer at his laptop. "A spreadsheet?" The *ugh* is implied.

"There's going to be more than one task at a time, and how will we decide which one to work on?"

"Whichever one gets us the most points, right?"

Marco shrugs. "Something might be worth more points,

but maybe there are more opportunities for creativity, or maybe it'll be further away from us than two tasks nearby of equal or more points."

He starts making a table, columns at the top labeled *task, estimated time, distance, difficulty,* etc. I lean against him and watch, his fingers deftly moving around the keyboard. Then he switches tabs over to the Discord server, which still has just one thing visible: a giant clock counting down. We have eighteen minutes left until the clock hits zero and we'll get more information.

Marco lifts his head, eyes searching the room. "Wasn't there an information sheet with the toys? Did it say how many points this task nets us?"

I slip off the couch and bend over, digging into the box. There's still supplies in here—scissors, tape. I guess they assume we have nothing helpful. Level the playing field or something.

I find what I'm looking for and grab the sheet. I straighten and spin around, Marco's eyes looking up from where I was digging around to my face. I wave the paper. "Found it. Okay, let's see." I scan the sheet, which has the address and some tips as I walk back to the couch.

If the toy or packaging breaks, call . . .

Deliver the wrapped toys to . . .

Drop a photo of both team members with the wrapped gifts in . . .

"Aha." I plop down next to Marco, accidentally sitting closer than I intended. My knee nudges the laptop and I fold my leg, my foot going underneath my butt, my knee resting on Marco's thigh.

He doesn't seem to notice.

I frown. "Two points? That can't be right." I glance up at the pile of presents. "Two measly points for wrapping all of this?"

Marco frowns too and leans into me, looking at the paper.

"That's what it says. The activity points can total up to sixty, plus another forty possible judges' points. We have three days; assuming roughly an even distribution over the days, that's twenty points per day."

"So wait. Billy Bob has made a pledge for every point that we earn, right? How much per point are we earning for charity here? What's our time worth?"

The keyboard clacks as Marco adds another two columns to the spreadsheet. *Actual time* and *Dollars raised per hour.* Then I watch over his shoulder as he clicks around to his browser, then his email, and opens the PDF of our sign-up form.

I leap to my feet. "Whoa! Holy bananas!"

Marco holds up a hand. "Easy. That's a mistake." He squints at the PDF, where Billy Bob handwrote a two and four zeroes on the pledge line. "Maybe. Probably. Do you think he meant twenty dollars and zero cents? Like he's missing the decimal?"

"If the total points available is a hundred, I was thinking that people would pledge, like . . . ten dollars. Or less. But also Billy Bob is fucking rich. He probably wipes his ass with twenties."

"He has a twenty-five-thousand-dollar bidet," Marco says absently while he types the number into his spreadsheet. "If we were to get all hundred points—"

"Which is impossible."

"We'd be raising two hundred thousand dollars for charity."

"Holy shit," I laugh. I imagine all my debt wiped out in one go, with some left over to get my own apartment so I don't have to accept Marco's charity anymore. It seems impossible that with a simple swipe of a pen, Billy Bob's just going to *give away* a life-changing amount of money.

Marco's face scrunches up and he tilts his head all the way to hit the back of the couch. "I feel like working with William has made me out of touch with these kinds of things. Is this a lot of money for William? No. But is this a lot of money for a charity organization? Probably. Right?"

He looks at me like I have an answer. I shrug, palms out to the side. I *wish* I had a thousand dollars to throw around to charity, and that's a fraction of what William pledged.

"They haven't said anything about what the average pledge amount is, right?" I ask. "Or if there's a minimum or maximum?"

I sit back down and we scroll the form. Nada.

"Hold on." Marco pulls his phone out of his pocket and taps it a few times, and soon I hear ringing.

"Hey, man." A shudder goes through my body at the sound of Greg's voice.

"Quick question for you; how much did you get pledged for this game?"

"Feeling a competitive edge, are we?" He chuckles, and then tells us that his pledges are just under a thousand dollars.

"Why, what's yours?"

"I have to talk to William about it. This paperwork is messy."

Hmm. He dodged the question. Interesting.

"Well, we could make it more exciting," Greg drawls.

I scoff silently. Like this is going to be boring?

"What do you have in mind?" Marco asks.

"Hmm . . . what about the loser sets the winner up on a date with a friend of their choice. Like, say . . . if I win, you set me up on a date with your teammate?"

My eyes widen and I shake my head vigorously.

Marco frowns at his phone. "You gotta do that work yourself. I'm not pushing you on Brin."

Greg laughs. "Okay, fine. How about the loser has to be the winner's personal assistant for a week?"

Marco looks skeptical. "How would that work?"

"When you lose, you have to spend a week doing anything from my job that I can delegate to you, *plus* you have to do things to assist me. My laundry, errands, et cetera."

My roommate chuckles. "You mean when I win, you have to meal prep for me for a week, deep clean my running gear, and hand-pick William's rotating art collection."

I have to admit, I *really* like the idea of Greg hand-washing Marco's running shorts. And I know that picking art for William's apartment is Marco's least favorite job, because it requires taking a trip outside of the city to a climate-controlled storage facility and overseeing the art being packed up and then distributed around the house.

Three times.

Because even though Billy Bob gives absolutely zero guidance for what he's in the mood for, he has strong opinions and doesn't hesitate to make Marco do it over and over again.

"Don't hold your breath," Greg says. "What do you say, are we on?"

The guys quickly agree to their side deal.

When Marco hangs up, I turn on the couch to face him. "You didn't tell Greg how much William pledged. Why?"

"I think this is a mistake," Marco admits. "William must have put two zeros for cents in there. It doesn't make any sense."

"Do you think he is even going to notice the amount that gets donated?"

"No . . ." he says slowly, as if it's just now dawning on him.

"And if he gets upset, it's his own fault. You have the paperwork."

Marco rubs his face, thinking. "He did say he didn't expect me to do much. To paraphrase, I think he said, 'Show up, don't embarrass me.'"

"So if he expected so little of you, then it would make

sense that he would pledge that large of an amount. You do a couple of tasks, bada bing, bada boom, it's whatever." I duck down to look in Marco's eyes. "But . . . what if we won the contest? What if we got as close as we possibly could to a hundred points? It's for *charity*. We could win them *a lot* of money. And you know, it's the season of giving." I lilt my voice up in a tease, knowing it'll rile him.

Marco snorts. "The holidays are for commercialism and religious righteousness. Most charitable giving is token, and a mere pittance. Just look at William."

But he looks at the spreadsheet again. Any money William has pledged is just a fraction of his net worth. The charities deserve it, and even if it is small change to William, at least it's something.

"All right," Marco agrees. "Two thousand dollars it is."

As if punctuating the statement, the door to our apartment opens.

7

———

MARCO

Bea, clearly in a rush, kicks her shoes off, and I close my laptop.

Brin and I watch in amusement while a frazzled Bea packs for her weeklong trip to upstate New York. She gets even more frazzled when some guy named Charlie shows up at our door claiming she's giving him a ride.

But it's hard to keep focused, especially when Brin's still pressed up against me, watching our roommate's drama with wide eyes that ping-pong between the two of them.

When the door slams closed behind Bea and Charlie, Brin jumps up. "I've got to get ready for work. I guess you'll have to manage the present wrapping by yourself tonight."

"No problem," I say, and reopen my laptop. Brin walks into our room, leaving the door open a crack.

I pull the Discord server up again. "Oh hey," I call over my shoulder. "The countdown is over."

There is no longer a single channel, but multiple channels.

"Wait, wait, wait," Brin calls. I hear drawers opening and closing, the sound of clothes ruffling and then an "ahhhh!"

"Brin, you okay?"

"Don't come in! I'm putting pants on," she warns. I face

45

my laptop again and rub my forehead. She's not wearing pants. Logically, I already knew that, but to hear her say it puts a visual in my head.

Brin finally appears in the doorway. She's in her black pants and a sports bra, exposing her midriff to me. I rarely ever see her in this state of undress, and it's like I'm living in Victorian times and graced with seeing her ankles.

I know Brin is shy with her body, and I think she's just goddamn clueless about how sexy she is.

"So are there more tasks?" Brin perches on the couch, and I avoid looking at the softness of her stomach.

I click around. There's an FAQ channel—a quick scan reveals nothing we don't already know from the session today—an announcement channel, a general chat for people to ask questions, and then a team channel. The announcement channel already has a red number next to it, indicating there's an important new message.

I click it open. The first announcement was right at five, which included the list of open challenges that could be completed anytime. I copy and paste those over to my spreadsheet. There's a reminder to wrap presents and turn them in before sending a photo in as proof. Then there's the newest announcement, which Brin leans in to read over my shoulder:

@everyone: Welcome and let the games begin! Make sure you have notifications turned on for this Discord server, as this is the only way you'll hear about burst challenges. Good luck and we can't wait to see your pictures!

Brin claps her hands in excitement. "Go back to the list."

I do and angle the screen to face her. The activities are so full of holiday spirit, it makes my jaw ache. There's not just Christmas tasks, but seasonal and multicultural tasks too.

Each one has a number on it indicating how many points we'll get when we complete the task.

"I can't believe I have to work," Brin moans. "I want to do these things *now*." She slumps against me, too distracted by the excitement of the scavenger hunt to be self-conscious. Her head is on my shoulder, and I get a whiff of her hair. It makes me think of the shower I heard, and I'm instantly longing for her to stay home with me tonight.

And do these holiday-themed tasks.

What is *wrong* with me?

Brin sits up and sighs. "Okay, those holiday-week tips are calling my name." She stands, but then pauses, looking down at me and worrying her lip. "If you wanted, I could see about someone picking up my shifts this week."

I am so tempted.

"I was going to . . . well, I could use the money, but this *is* for charity."

Guilt flickers in my gut. Brin might pay less rent than I do, but it's still more than she paid before she met me. If she needs the money, she needs the money, and I can't jeopardize that. "No, no, it'll be fine. We have plenty of time to get activities done this week."

Brin nods and retreats back to our room to finish getting ready. I can tell she feels bad.

I shake my attraction off. My desire for her company is ridiculous. We spend so much time together, and I would never ask her to skip work and risk her job. She needs stability in her life, she needs to feel safe.

I would be a real asshole if I risked that.

8

BRIN

WHEN I SHUFFLE OUT INTO THE LIVING ROOM THE NEXT morning, Marco is wrapping presents again. A giant pile of presents.

"What . . . ?"

Marco glances up. "There was an announcement that we could come pick up more presents to wrap. I ran and grabbed them."

"'Ow many points?" I mumble.

"Six." He doesn't look up from his work.

My eyebrows raise. That's the most points we've seen for any one task, except for cutting down your own Christmas tree. We didn't even have to talk about nixing that one, though. Cutting down our own tree would be fun, but given how Marco's brother died, there's no way I want to subject Marco to that.

I have questions, but I'm not awake enough to think just yet, so I stumble into the kitchen. There's a cup of coffee waiting for me. Marco lets me perch on the un-present-piled side of the couch and wake up slowly.

There are scraps of wrapping paper and empty tubes all over the place. We're not being tidy, though it's hard to be too

49

focused on cleaning when we're just going to make a mess again.

Marco wraps a YA book, folding precise, neat edges, and then holding the paper down while he carefully rips a few inches of tape off the roll. He's wearing gray sweatpants again this morning—he has several pairs—with a *Heartstopper* tee. The edges of his hair are damp, curling, like he showered this morning.

I sit cross-legged and sip my coffee. Marco and I have the full day to rack up as many points as we can until I go into work.

I check my phone. It's already ten a.m., and there are a few unread announcements in the Discord server. We missed a burst challenge while I was sleeping—sledding.

I put the phone down. "How did you get all the presents here?"

"An UberXL."

"I would have helped."

"I know." He flashes me a quick smile. Then he stops wrapping a small stuffie and holds out his thumb. "Gave myself a paper cut."

There's a bright, angry red strip on the pad of his thumb. I lean forward, setting my coffee on the floor, and crawl toward him. It looks irritated but it's not bleeding. I grab his hand and pull it closer for inspection.

Then, just to be cute, I kiss the cut. "You'll live."

I expect him to laugh, but when I glance up, his Adam's apple is bobbing, his gaze darting between my lips, his thumb, and below my face.

Before I left our bedroom I threw on an old sweatshirt, a stretched-out, super soft Lookouts one, my dad's favorite minor league baseball team.

I did not put on a bra.

Mortified that Marco can see down my top, I panic and my arm gives out from underneath me. Marco's grip on my hand tightens and jerks up, like he's trying to save me, but this ship is going down.

I face-plant into the carpet.

"Jesus," Marco says. "Are you okay?"

One cheek is smooshed up so my lips are making a kissy face. "Mi'm finbe."

I am fine . . . just my dignity is in shambles. Whatever.

Marco helps me push back onto the couch and I take a huge swig of my barely-cool-enough-to-drink coffee. "Should I wrap presents?" I ask when I swallow. I think I've just burned my tongue.

He shakes his head. "I was thinking we could do one of the more creative ones. Something that has the potential to earn us a bunch of extra points."

I nod and pull out my phone. Marco's head bends back over the kid's camera he's wrapping.

Pulling up the spreadsheet, I start to read off the list. Marco and I discard a few tasks that are more physical instead of creative. We debate how to go about making the biggest paper snowflake that we can, but ultimately decide on the one that we think will get us to most creative points— holiday-themed culinary art.

"It has to be edible and at least one square foot in size," I read.

"What if we went down to that candy store and bought red and green M&M's and did something like a mural or mosaic?" Marco suggests.

I wrinkle my nose. "That might have to be really big to make recognizable shapes."

We go to the candy store anyway, and see what they have. We walk out twenty minutes later with a giant bag of knock-off Starbursts in bright red, yellow, and green. We'll use them like Play-Doh to create a Christmas tree at the suggestion of the store clerk.

I pull one of the individually wrapped green candies out

of the bag as we walk to the subway and frown at it. "I wonder why Starburst doesn't have a green." I unwrap the bright green cube and pop it into my mouth.

It's mint.

"Bleh." I spit the whole piece out.

"What is it?" Marco says, laughter in his voice. "Green apple? Lime?"

"Mint," I say. Ugh, I've just drooled all over my hand. I trot over to a trash can and throw the vile candy away and wipe my hand on the side of my fleece-lined yoga pants. When Marco catches up, I stick out my tongue. "Gross."

He shakes his head. We both dodge piles of gray slush on the sidewalk as we walk back to our place. I just threw sneakers on but I regret not wearing my boots. Today is sunny and warm enough that everything is wet and cold and dreary.

We stop at Duane Reade for posterboard and when we get home, we dump all the candy on our kitchen table and set to work peeling the candies and shaping them. I put on Christmas music, starting with "HERE (for Christmas)" by Lukas Graham, which always makes me cry. I belt out the lyrics while I twist yellow candies into ornaments and Marco hums along next to me. It's kinda sticky work, and it definitely puts me off eating Starbursts.

Ding!

Both our phones go off at the same time and we freeze and look up at each other. Marco abandons his pile of green smooshed candy and picks up his phone. "It's another burst challenge," he says, excitement spilling into the words.

I drop the candy. "What do we do?"

Marco's quiet while he reads the announcement. Then he glances up at me. "We have ten minutes to send a picture of a kiss under mistletoe."

9

MARCO

go! Get your shoes on!"

It's a good thing she can think, because my head is filled with *kiss under mistletoe, kiss under mistletoe, kiss under mistletoe* . . .

We scramble to throw sneakers and jackets on before we careen down the stairs. I can take them two at a time, so I beat Brin to the door. "Which way?" I'm already breathless as I hold the door open for her.

"Left!" she shrieks, laughing as she passes me.

As I run behind her I start to think that maybe this isn't the best idea. What good can come from kissing my roommate?

"How many points is it?" Brin asks. She's slowed a little, and I keep pace with her.

I check my phone, trying to focus my eyes on the screen. "Five," I read. Brin picks up the pace again. "It says only one team member needs to be in the picture, and it doesn't have to be on the lips."

"Five points as long as there's a kiss and mistletoe. Easy."

"Where are we going?"

"There's a bodega over by the Whole Foods that has mistletoe."

I huff. I run every day, but usually not wearing a full winter jacket and sweatpants. I'm starting to sweat. But at Brin's words, my feet start to feel like lead.

Brin, who does not work out at all, is breathing hard next to me. "I noticed it last week and thought it was super romantic. I mean, I've seen the couple that runs the place—" She stops talking to catch her breath.

Is this really what I want? To kiss Brin for the first time in a random bodega, with me sweating under my jacket and her shoe soaked and soggy while some stranger takes a picture of us?

I'm just about to open my mouth and say that five points isn't worth it when Brin skids to a stop and pushes her way into the bodega. "Almost missed it!" she cries over her shoulder. Then she's pointing triumphantly above her. I look up and there it is, a single sprig of mistletoe hanging above the vestibule.

I stare at it. This is not what I want.

"Excuse me," Brin says, and I watch, frozen, as she approaches the bodega's shopkeeper, a Korean woman in her fifties. Brin holds out her phone. "Would you take a video of us kissing under the mistletoe?"

The lady eyes us. "Mistletoe for customers only."

"We're customers." Brin grabs a handful of flavored chip bags from nearby and bounces impatiently while the woman rings them up.

I scan the bodega. There's only one other customer here, a sixty-something Black man with a beard and salt-and-pepper hair under a fedora.

So it's me, the shopkeeper, or the old man.

Who am I kidding? I obviously can't ask Brin to kiss a stranger.

The old man catches my eye. "Hey." I give him an up-chin. "Five dollars to let me kiss you on the cheek under the mistletoe."

Brin whips around. "What?"

I hold up my hands. "No funny business. We're just doing this scavenger hunt and we need—"

"Why you don't want to kiss me?" the shopkeeper demands.

Brin holds up her phone, and I can see the countdown, which has less than two minutes. "What are you doing, Marco? Just kiss me and we can get it over with."

Get it over with? This is just getting worse and worse.

"Twenty dollars," I tell the old man.

He raises an eyebrow. "I think you're spoken for, young man." Huh, he even sounds like James Earl Jones. "Kiss the girl."

"Kiss her. Kiss her. Kiss her," the shopkeeper chants.

Brin fumbles with her phone, navigating to the camera, and hands it to the shopkeeper. "It's on video, just point it at us."

The shopkeeper holds it up, too focused on the camera work to chant, so at least that's over.

Brin bounces up to me, frozen on the spot under the mistletoe. The minute our eyes meet, though, she pauses. "Unless . . . unless *you* don't want to?"

"I . . ." I shake my head. "No, it's fine." It's five points. Totally fine. I can do this. I can even get creative with it.

This sends Brin bouncing on her toes again. "Sweet! This is gonna get us so many points." She slings an arm over my shoulder. "It's just a peck. Nothing fancy. We just have to— whoa!"

I pull a move I've seen on TikTok. I bend into her, sweeping my opposite hand behind her knees. Her arm tightens around my shoulder as I pull her into a bridal carry and she squeals in delight.

And then we kiss. Our timing's off, so my lips close in a

kiss just as she's pulling away, and her mouth hits a bit off center from mine, but that's fine.

It totally counts as a kiss.

Our first kiss.

We hold awkwardly until the shopkeeper says, "Got it."

Brin squirms to be let down and rushes to the counter. With a few taps she has uploaded the video to the channel, and then turns the countdown clock to me.

00:10

00:09

00:08

She turns it back and grins at me. "We made it. Okay, let's get home. My foot is *freezing!*"

10

BRIN

MARCO IS DEAD QUIET ON THE WALK BACK TO OUR APARTMENT. In all the excitement of the last ten minutes I started sweating, so I fan my sweatshirt out from my chest the first block, but then the chilly air cools me down too fast, and I start to get cold.

Having a soaked-through sneaker doesn't help either. I'm squelching with every step and my toes are going numb.

Now that the excitement of the mega-points-winning has worn off, I'm second-guessing the whole interaction. I tried to remain as cool as possible. Just a kiss, no big deal, right?

I did it for the points! For charity! My stupid little heart that fluttered when Marco's lips hit mine can shut the hell up.

It was just a peck on the lips with my roommate, one of the people I know best in the world. Marco is not helping, because he's trodding along silently behind me.

Did I just force myself on him? I didn't think it would be that big of a deal.

Another part of me is offended. It's just a kiss! Get over it. I'm reasonably attractive and it didn't mean anything.

I surreptitiously exhale into my palm. I don't even have bad breath!

Inside our apartment I toe my shoe off and make a face at the soggy mess of my right sneaker. I sit on the couch and peel off my sock.

"Jesus Christ," Marco says. "Your toes are blue."

"It's not that bad," I insist, but Marco kneels down in front of me anyway. He picks my foot up and rubs his hands over it, one on the sole of my foot and one on the top. I jerk away and giggle. "Hey!"

Marco holds up his hands. "I know, I know." He rolls his eyes. "I wasn't trying to tickle you." He shifts his attention to my toes.

Okay, the big one is a little pale. It's not *blue.*

Marco rubs my toes more aggressively and then knits his fingers together, pressing my foot between his hands and making a toe sandwich. His hands are warm and slightly calloused from his time at the gym. But I have always loved his hands, with their trim, neat nails and the light dusting of hair on the back.

We sit like this for a few more moments. Marco's thumb lightly runs over the side of my toe, careful not to tickle me again. His dark hair has fallen forward onto his forehead, and his brow is slightly wrinkled in concentration. I warm from the inside out, basking in having his attention so focused on making me feel good.

Even if it's just warming me up.

Marco breaks the quiet by letting go of my foot and leaning back. "Better?"

I wiggle my toes. "Yeah. I think this calls for a hot cocoa though. Then we can get back to work on the art."

Marco rises to his feet. "Let me get you some socks first. And where did your slippers go?"

I direct Marco to the kitchen, where I had abandoned my slippers under the table when we ran out to the bodega. He drops them at my feet. "And socks?"

"The bottom drawer of my nightstand."

I pull my feet underneath me to the edge of the couch and inspect my pedicure. I painted them at home, using one of my few splurges—a bottle of nail polish.

I hear the drawer to my nightstand slide open just in time to remember that I keep my hot pink vibrating dildo in my sock drawer. Mortification barrels through me, turning my cheeks hot and making me cringe. Even though Eva assures me most women own one, I'm still not over this hang-up. And that just doubles my embarrassment, because I wish I could be confident and brush it off.

Between the awkward kiss today and this, I feel less like an adult than before. What must Marco think of me?

11

BRIN

MARCO RETURNS WITH A PAIR OF SOCKS AND KNEELS BACK DOWN at my feet. My face is beet-red, but Marco doesn't say anything.

He tugs one sock on in silence, and then he's about to put the second one on but I can't stand the silence anymore.

"I'm so sorry! I forgot it was in there."

He pauses briefly but then works the sock over my toes. "You forgot what was in there?"

"Uh." Oh crap. Have I just put my foot in my mouth? "Nothing."

The sock is on now, and Marco releases me. I slip my feet into my slippers.

"In the drawer? Did I miss something?" He stands and takes a step toward our bedroom.

"Wait, no, it's nothing!" I grab his arm.

"No, now I've got to go look. I must have missed something." He tries to pull away from me, so I brace myself on the arm of the couch.

"It's nothing. Don't! You can't invade my privacy!"

"You're hiding something in there with your socks and your giant pink dildo?"

I'm so surprised—and mortified—I let go of Marco and he collapses against the doorjamb, laughing.

"I don't—why are you—it's not *giant!*" I cover my face with my hands. I really don't think it's that big, but I've only seen three dicks in my life in person so what do I know?

My roommate straightens. "Relax, I already knew you had it."

I look up at him. "You did?"

"Yeah. The night you moved in with me I saw you try to sneak it into a box."

"Oh my god." I put my face in my hands again.

"I also saw you try to discreetly throw away a few other toys," Marco admits.

"Well I couldn't fit everything in the boxes we had," I explain.

"I know," Marco says, sobering. But then he teases me again. "Sorry you had to make sacrifices."

I toss a throw pillow at him. "I'm so embarrassed."

"Don't be," he says. "I would think it was weirder if you didn't have a toy, to be honest. And I've got my own collection, too, so nothing to be embarrassed about."

That mollifies me—but also has me wondering what toys Marco has. I'm not even sure what the options are for guys, but I will definitely be doing some googling later.

We get back to the business of earning points. Marco makes us hot cocoa and we sit at the kitchen table to drink it, working on our candy Christmas tree.

The weird kiss with Marco doesn't leave my mind, though. I have to tell someone. While Eva's the most sex-positive person I know, Bea is also the most practical. Bea and I don't normally have girl chat, but I've been hoping to get her to join us at Eva's brunches, so maybe this would help to open up to her first.

BRIN

You won't believe the week we've been having. We'll tell you all about it when you get home. Hope you're enjoying the time with your family.

XOXO

Brin and Marco

PS: I may have gotten too much into the holiday spirit and kissed Marco. Argh! What was I thinking?

BEA

I am having a great time. Enjoy your days off and I'll see you soon.

PS. Wait. Am I supposed to be surprised that you kissed him, or surprised that you haven't been secretly banging this whole time?

I get that people think we are hooking up since we share a room together. But I think if we didn't share a room—if I didn't *need* to share a room—it would be more likely that something would ever happen between us. Someday, when I'm on better ground, maybe . . .

I don't know what I would want to happen, and I can't even begin to dream about it when I still feel so down in the trenches. I react with a surprised face emoji and put my phone back down.

After our edible art is done, we move onto the presents while we have some time before we leave.

There's a single activity on the list worth six points: attending a school play. Yesterday in the Discord server, someone had created a thread compiling a list of all the plays in the tristate area, and we'd chosen one that worked with my schedule at the restaurant and conveniently wasn't Christmas-centered or overly religious—more *Love, Actually* holiday show than a nativity concert at a cathedral.

It's out in the Bronx, in the afternoon, so we can fit it in before I go to work. On the subway, I swing gently side to side. There's an elderly Asian person busking, playing "O Holy Night" on a stringed instrument that sits across their lap, also taking up the seat next to them. No one seems to mind, though, and the tune comes out in a hauntingly beautiful, mournful melody.

I look around the subway car, to the middle-aged woman wearing menorah earrings, to the old man wearing a Christmas sweater, to the group of young people with numerous piercings carrying potluck dishes and each sporting the Pride flag in one way or another. This is so different from the little town I grew up in—I didn't know any Jewish people and the biggest church was conservative Catholic and my mom and her friends would have been scandalized to see a rainbow flag.

If I had gone home this year, like I did last year, I would be headed to church tonight to appease my mom. I'd be listening to a service about the Holy Family being a model for Christian values and how babies are a gift from God. The church would be offering meals to those who need it—with a side of sermon. I'd be listening to people who wouldn't love Marco and wouldn't have loved his brother because they're queer.

Even thinking about it breaks my heart a little.

Our stop is next, so Marco and I make our way to the doors. Marco tosses a bill into the busker's open instrument case, and I grab on to his jacket as the train sways to a stop.

Out on the street, Marco navigates us to the school, and we join the stream of families filtering into the auditorium. We take two free seats and the obligatory selfie of us with the stage to send in to claim our points.

And then the lights dim, and the show begins right away with a song called "What Do You Celebrate?," an upbeat number performed by about twenty kids. They sing the song and point to various decorations around the stage. Teachers parade past, holding up paper lanterns and menorahs and drums. Electric candles of all colors line the stage.

The audience claps along, swaying and singing the chorus. Even Marco claps, and I nudge him until he mouths the words along with the rest of us.

When that banger finishes, there's thunderous applause.

"Holy shit," I say. "I didn't know we were in for such a party."

A man steps out onto the stage, holding his hands up until the audience quiets, and he introduces the program and the next song, "Winter White Hymnal." A line of teenagers stands, hands over their hearts, and together they pat their chests. The mics pick it up, and a lone singer starts the first lyrics, the rest joining in one by one. The melody is beautiful, another haunting song that reminds me of the busker on the subway. This song is a cappella, nothing but their voices and claps.

There are four more songs, some instrumental and performed by members of the school's band. Others have backing tracks and are more lyrically focused. Some quiet and low, others upbeat.

One of the quiet and low songs is about coming home, about being loved, no matter where you come from and how you identify. It's then that I look over and see a tear falling down Marco's cheek.

He feels my gaze and glances at me before swiping it away. I dig into my purse and find a travel pack of tissues, offering him one. He takes it and wipes his face. When it disappears into his coat pocket, I reach over and thread my fingers through his, squeezing his hand as we watch the rest of the show.

———

When the performance is over, we rise, still holding hands, and follow the stream of happy families out of the theater.

Our fingers are intertwined and my heart is thudding. My flushed cheeks sting when I exit the building and run smack into the biting wind in the late afternoon.

Marco and I split from the crowd and walk a few blocks. Right before the subway station, there's a small park: bare branches, drooping pines, and a dry fountain. I use my hand to steer him toward the empty space, and he follows obediently.

When we're alone, standing before a bench that I don't really want to sit on because I know the cold will cut right through my pants, I turn toward Marco and slide my arms around his waist. Marco's not a big hugger, but something right now tells me he needs it.

He freezes for a moment. Have I made a huge mistake? But then he collapses over me, embracing my shoulders and letting his chin drop to the top of my head. His coat is open, so when I burrow into him, it wraps around me, tucking us into a cocoon. Marco's heart beats steadily under my cheek.

Buh-bum. Buh-bum. Buh-bum.

We stand like that for a long time. So long that when I open my eyes, there's a dusting of snow on his lapel. I nestle in deeper and count his heartbeats.

One . . . two . . .

"Did I ever tell you why I came to the city?" Marco's voice rumbles.

I shake my head as much as I can while being pressed against his chest. I know Marco grew up in Long Island, but he's been here for at least a decade.

"When I was sixteen, my brother was home from NYU for the holidays. He was staying in the basement, and Christmas Eve my dad walked in and caught him blowing an old high school friend. My parents flipped their shit. They kicked him out that night, nothing but the clothes on his back. They stopped paying for his school, so he had to drop out."

Marco's voice is stronger now. "Joe tried so hard to get them to talk to him again. He begged my parents. He pleaded. He told them it was a mistake. And then one night I realized I hadn't heard from him in a month. My parents never talked about him. I was terrified."

I squeeze him tighter, wishing I could close my ears so I don't have to hear about what happened to Marco's brother.

"I spent six weeks going into the city as much as I could, looking for him. I skipped school. I checked shelters. I talked to the university, the police."

Even though I know that Marco finds him, and they live together until Joe's death, I'm nervous and tense. How could Marco's family splinter like that?

"When I finally found him he was living in the Meat-packing District in a loft with, like, six other people. I was so goddamn happy to have found him. And I was so mad at my parents, so I ran away and went to live with Joe. Of course, it ticked my parents off even more, but I could see that Joe needed me. He'd been kicked out of leases, lost jobs; he was too nice."

I smile against his chest. Marco is always telling me I'm too nice, just like his brother.

He continues. "We found our place here in the city. We found our people." Marco jerks his head back in the direction we came from. "How can our world be so divided that some people are teaching their kids to love and accept everyone, and yet my parents can't even be in the same house with their own queer son?"

I squeeze him. I don't have an answer. To me, this world we live in, where our families can't see past their own bigotry, is unexplainable.

"Thank you for being here with me," Marco says, and I feel the press of his lips on my hair.

"You're welcome. I'm here for hugs and art projects and kisses under the mistletoe."

I feel it in my bones when he lets out a small laugh. "You mean our terrible first kiss?"

And then underneath my arms Marco freezes.

I pull back and look up at him. "Our *first* kiss?" My lips curl up and I tease him, my heart beating faster in my chest. "Are there going to be more?"

"Come on." He huffs a laugh, looking away. The snow's still falling around us in light little flakes, enough to add a wintery sparkle to the air. "You don't want to kiss a guy like me."

"Well, it was a pretty terrible first kiss," I drawl. "Why would I want a second one?"

Marco's eyes meet mine, sharp now, narrowed on me. "That was a terrible kiss because we were rushed and being watched by complete strangers. *Being filmed.*"

"You don't think it's because we're two completely incompatible heights? Fundamentally unable to kiss comfortably?"

His gaze drops down. Somehow, despite the obvious height difference, our faces have gotten closer.

"No, I don't. We may be incompatible in other ways, but it's not your pocket-sized stature that holds us back." He takes a breath, and I feel it all over my body, from the expansion of his ribs to the warmth unfurling across my cheeks. "In fact, I don't think there's anything physical about us that's incompatible."

My heels are off the ground, my toes pressing into the dirt.

He doesn't stop. His eyes, always dark, are half-lidded black pools. "I think if we wanted to, we could have an exceptional second kiss."

I swallow, and my eyes drop to his mouth. "If we wanted to," I agree. I lick my lips and his gaze follows. This is bad. Everything I've ever felt, all the yearning and pent-up frustration, is overriding all the reasons why I shouldn't be risking my living situation, the tiny amount of financial security that I have right now, like this. All I know is that I want to kiss him.

A flare of a memory from earlier today pops into my head: Marco looking for a reason *not* to kiss me under the mistletoe. The way he was quiet and reserved afterward.

"You didn't want to kiss me this morning," I say.

"No."

Our noses are almost touching. I'm having a hard time focusing on anything but his lips.

"Why not?"

He gazes at me, studying my face, while I look up at him. When he speaks again, his voice is rough. "Because I wanted our first kiss to be something more like this."

It's so soft, at first. His lips barely brush mine, and my eyes flutter closed. His kiss gets firmer with each pass, our lips not even breaking apart. There's no end, just a continuous roll of our breaths mingling together, my mouth softening under his. His tongue teases with a gentleness that makes my knees weak. Marco's arms slide down as I open to him, pulling me up, pressing me harder against him. I'm barely on my toes and Marco's arms, his body, curl around me.

And then it's deep and plundering. I let out a moan and Marco answers. Fire flicks up my insides, my whole body responding to his. I can feel him hard against my belly and I press my hips forward, purposefully grinding against him.

Marco groans again, one hand banding me to him and the other in my hair, holding me to him. I'm bent back, my hands inside his jacket, wrapping around his back and clawing at him, desperate for more contact.

Simultaneously, our phones buzz. Marco's is in his jacket pocket, so it vibrates against my shoulder, while mine is in my purse against my hip.

We pull back, my feet hitting the ground, and cold air rushes between us. Marco's lips are swollen, and I swallow hard. I let go of him, raising my fingers to my lips to feel their matching tenderness.

Have we just jeopardized our friendship, our living situation? If Marco knew how much of a mess my life was, he wouldn't be kissing me. He probably wouldn't even want to be roommates with me anymore, because I'm one lost job away from drowning, from needing *more* of his charity.

And that's something I'll never let happen again.

12

MARCO

I'm afraid I'm going to fuck up my relationship with Brin. I have a history, after all, of ruining relationships with people who are important to me.

It's not too late, I remind myself. It was one kiss.

One spectacularly hot kiss.

Oh shut up, brain. You're an asshole, just like the rest of me.

"That was probably dumb, wasn't it?" Brin looks up at me.

"Oh god." I squeeze my eyes closed. Brin has so much to lose here, I *know* that. She works so goddamn hard and the last thing she needs is me fucking up her living situation by making everything uncomfortable. "I'm sorry—"

"I'm sorry too. That was—"

"—I shouldn't have done that—"

"—a really bad idea—"

"—because I like our living situation."

"Yeah." Brin bites her lip. "I do too. And as epic as that kiss was, I'm not dating, you know, or . . ."

"Yeah, yeah, I know. And"—I rub the back of my neck—"it's chemistry, obviously. We're friends. We like each other."

"Chemistry," Brin echoes. "I don't have a whole lot of experience in that department." She waves her hands between us.

"Is this"—I mimic her hand gesture—"kissing your roommate? Or is it . . ." I give her a skeptical look. "Kissing in general?"

When I stare at her, Brin gives a nervous laugh. "Kissing in general."

"Have you—"

We both talk at the same time. I say, "Had sex?" and she says, "Yeah."

Then we do it again, this time with me saying, "Oh, okay" and her saying, "Oh wait. Sex? No."

"Hang on." I put a hand up to stop us from talking over each other. "Are you a virgin?"

"Well, not in the sense of like . . ." She makes a hand gesture that clearly means penetration.

Surprisingly, I get what she's not saying. "Sorry," I say, rubbing my jaw. "Virgin probably isn't the best word. The patriarchy is weird about what defines virginity and really limits it to the heterosexuals, anyway. There's a lot of great sex that's not 'sex.'"

She laughs.

Plus, Brin's got that toy in the nightstand, one that definitely looks like its main function is penetration.

What exactly do you say to someone who's told you they've never had sex before? *Especially* right after you've kissed them?

"Thank you for sharing that with me," I say. "You're right, it's probably not the best idea. Because we live together. And I *really* like living with you."

I can tell Brin's cheeks are flushed, even in the dark, but at least now it's more from the flattery than embarrassment.

I take a step back and pull my phone out of the pocket. I'd almost forgotten that it had buzzed. The screen is bright in the dark night and there's a new notice in the server.

@everyone: The next burst challenge is this: The shortest day of the year is tomorrow. Honor the solstice by taking a picture of <u>both team members</u> watching the sunrise. Upload it by eight am.

There's more information, and I read the whole thing out loud to Brin.

"What time is sunrise?" she asks after I'm done.

I google it. "A little after seven. It would mean a really early morning after you work close tonight."

"How many points is it worth?"

"Three."

Brin makes her thinking face. I'm glad we have something to distract us from that kiss. Having a practical problem to figure out is much better than worrying over whether I completely fucked things up with Brin. "That means I would get like . . . four hours of sleep?"

"Plus we have to get somewhere where we can actually see the sunrise."

"We could take the ferry? Or Pier 17?"

"Yeah . . . or we can go up to William's penthouse."

Brin wrinkles her nose. "We can do that?"

I shrug. "Sure. He's not home."

Her eyes widen and she puts a hand to her forehead dramatically. "You'll spoil me. What if I become accustomed to a life of penthouse suites and sunrise views?"

This is better. We kissed, it was dumb, we moved on. Something inside me unwinds. I don't have to worry about being yet another person who's taken advantage of Brin.

"We'll have to move to a place with a better view," I banter back.

"Ha. Like that'll happen." Brin turns and starts walking in the direction of the subway. "Okay, I guess I'm in. You're responsible for setting the alarm and bringing me coffee though."

"Deal."

13

MARCO

When my alarm goes off the next day, the soft buzzing of my smartwatch waking me up, I roll over and look at Brin, just like I do most mornings.

Last night's kissing debacle definitely infused some weirdness between us, but it was nothing a little space couldn't fix. Brin went to work and I ordered kung pao chicken and watched an action movie.

I'm not a total monster who would take advantage of his roommate. I didn't irreparably damage my friendship with Brin, even if I lay awake in bed thinking about that kiss—the way her lips felt on mine, how she opened up to me, her smell . . .

And the fact that she'd never had sex before.

I dreamed about kissing her more and exploring how far she'd want to go.

And woke up hard.

Totally fine. We'll get over it, rack up a bunch of points today, and be right back to normal.

Despite the chill in the air, her covers are halfway down her body, exposing her white tank top and peaked nipples.

God, why am I always noticing her nipples?

There's a slip of skin showing above the waistband of her boxers that she wears to bed—she pulled out her holiday ones the day after Thanksgiving, and today's have candy canes and mistletoe on a bright green background. Her hair is a red halo around her face, and one arm is thrown over her head while she breathes softly.

Most mornings when I wake up before her, I tiptoe around, picking up the clothes I set out the night before and sneaking into the bathroom down the hall for my daily quiet jerk-off ritual before I get ready for the day. But today I sit up, putting my feet on the floor and noisily stretching, overexaggerating my yawn.

I've never had to wake her up before. We both have our own schedules, our own independence, so this is new territory.

Brin stirs but doesn't wake.

I crouch down to eye level, the cotton of my sweatpants straining over my thighs. "Brin," I say softly. "It's six. Time to wake up."

I've never been this close to a sleeping Brin.

She sighs and turns to her side, curling up and pushing her face into the pillow.

"Brin." I'm louder now, and I run my hand up her arm to her shoulder and cup it.

She grunts.

I shake her gently.

"Naaa . . . whaaa . . . fuuuu?" One arm reaches out from under the pillow and lightly pops me in the face. I sputter while she feels around, as if looking for a snooze button. Not finding one, her hand settles on my shoulder, curling around the bare muscle and pulling me closer.

She finally turns her face toward me and I see one sky-blue eye crack open and blink at me. I tilt my head, matching the angle of hers.

"Marco?" Her hand squeezes and then drops, fingers

trailing over my pec and through the hair on my chest. She makes a soft little noise, a hum, and something curls inside my gut.

Her fingers trace lower, and lower . . .

Her eyes are closed again, and her hand drops to dangle off the bed.

I sigh, and then I grab her hand and shake it back and forth. "Brin!"

Her eyes fly open and I drop her hand. She blinks at me for a moment before turning onto her back to stretch. Cool air floods in where her touch had been and I instantly miss it. But when she's done stretching, she turns to face me again. "What time is it?" She blinks.

"Six," I repeat. "Remember, we're watching the sun rise for the scavenger hunt?"

She hums again and closes her eyes.

"Nope, come on, get up." I grab her closest hand and tug harder. "If we can get out the door within the next ten minutes I'll have time to make you an espresso at William's place."

Brin doesn't answer, but rolls toward me and off the bed, barely giving me time to get out of the way before she stands, toe to toe with me. She stretches again and yawns so wide I can count her back teeth before she slumps against me, face-first, into my chest.

I laugh, causing her head to bounce, and lightly wrap my arms around her.

This is new. This is weird. This is causing my heart rate to sky rocket because she's in that skimpy little tank top and a pair of boxers with the waistband rolled up and I'm only wearing my worn gray sweatpants and I can feel her hard nipples and her hot breath and . . .

Brin straightens, blinks sluggishly, and walks toward the door like a zombie. I hear her trundle down the hall and into the bathroom, leaving me standing in the middle of the bedroom with a growing hard-on and an ache in my chest.

I shake it off and get dressed while Brin's in the bathroom. I knock after five minutes. "Brin. Five more minutes for the espresso offer."

Ten seconds later there's a flush, then I hear the water running. The door opens and I switch places with a still-groggy Brin. A few minutes later I'm by the door, waiting, while she changes clothes with the door cracked open while I try not to look.

With seven seconds left to spare, Brin comes out in jeans and a cranberry-red sweater. I hold out my hand and she grabs it, using it for balance while she tugs on her waterproof sheep-skin-lined boots that I got her last year for Christmas. I retrieve her knit beanie which she tugs over her head, covering the bun she'd pulled her hair back into. I wrestle her into a jacket and lead the way down the stairs.

The whole trip, Brin is half-asleep. I take us to the right subway, hook my arms around her when she sways on the ride, and when she gets cold despite the layers she's wearing, I give her my coat. She burrows into it, her closed eyes the only thing visible while I brace against the motion of the train.

When we get to William's place, I wave to the security guard and Brin and I ride the elevator up. I park her out on the balcony while I make that espresso I promised her with William's fancy machine.

When I get back outside, Brin is asleep on the lounge chair. That's fine, the coffee is too hot anyway. I set our coffees down on the wicker table next to her and grab a blanket from inside and cover her up.

When I sit down on the other side of the lounger, Brin shifts slightly and I look at her.

"Are you awake?" I whisper. "There's coffee."

Instead of rolling away from me for the coffee, she rolls

toward me. Her eyes blink open and she does that adorable lip-smacking thing again. "Wake me up . . . for the picture." And then she buries her face in my shoulder.

"Hang on," I say, and try to extract my arm from underneath her. She grunts in annoyance. "Hang *on*."

Finally my arm is free and I put it around her. Brin sighs in happiness and wiggles closer.

That little sigh echoes inside me. I've got a beautiful woman snuggling up against me. My boss is gone for the week, my coffee is within reach, and the sky is a brilliant golden-red hue. There are clouds out, enough to keep it interesting without blocking the view, although behind us, low gray clouds loom.

I take my phone out and, even though Brin's not awake and the sun's not up yet, I take a few pictures. I want to remember this. A rare good moment when the holidays are usually shit.

The sunrise continues to bloom and when I finally catch the first dot of molten gold from the sun, I shake Brin awake.

"Whu—?"

"It's time. We gotta get up."

Brin rolls and stretches and then I pull her to her feet. We both turn our backs to the railing and I hold the phone out and angle it to get both our faces and the sunrise. Some of her hair has come loose from the beanie and the wind whips it around and she shivers. I pull her tighter and then *click*, it's done.

"All right, another three points in the book," I say. I navigate to the private team channel for us to upload our proof of points and send the picture. Then I update our spreadsheet. We have twenty-six points now.

"Hmmmm . . ." When I look down at Brin, she's horizontal on the lounger again.

"Hey," I say, reaching down to grab her foot and shake it. "Your coffee is getting cold."

"Don't want coffee," she mumbles. "More sleep."

"You'll sleep better if we get you home to your own bed. Then you can sleep all you want and I'll work on more tasks. Like . . ." I think for a minute. "Baking cookies."

That gets me an eye blinking open and an exaggerated pout. "But I wanted to bake Christmas cookies. You don't even *like* Christmas cookies."

"I like two more points for our team. And then you can eat cookies when you wake up."

Her eyes close again, either not sold on the idea of eating my cookies or falling victim to the comfortable lounger.

"Oh no you don't." I grab her ankle and lift her foot up.

Brin sits up in protest, instantly waking up a bit more. "Whoa. No need to do anything hasty."

I wrestle her boot off. "Marco," she warns. "Don't do it." She tries to tug her foot away but my grip is too solid.

"I'm sitting here thinking, what would wake you up even more than coffee? After all, coffee has this horrible flaw that you have to actually transport it to your mouth." Her boot comes off and I have a free hand to mime drinking coffee. "That sounds too hard for you first thing in the morning."

"Marco!"

I hook that foot under my arm, facing away from her, and pinch the toe of her sock. "But this seems like an effective method." With a smooth tug, the sock comes off.

Brin thrashes now in earnest, already laughing even though I haven't touched her foot yet. I only accidentally discovered that the soles of her feet are super ticklish a few months ago.

"Marco, I'm awake, I'm awake!"

I trace the lightest touch of my finger down the center of her sole and she convulses and squeals. Next thing I know, she's tackling me from behind, trying to grab my wrists and pry me away with one hand while her other hand covers my eyes. She pokes me in my right eye, but it's a small price to pay. Her laughter is right in my ear, loud and ringing and infectious.

"All right, all right," I say, and let go of her foot, shifting to grip her thighs through her pajama pants before standing up with her on my back like a monkey. She stops wiggling, and instead rests her head on my shoulder. I bend over, careful not to drop her, and pick up her sock and shoe. I leave the coffee mugs . . . I'll clean them up before William gets home.

"Ew, you're touching my dirty sock."

"You put it on like an hour ago, how dirty can it be?" I huff.

"A dirty sock is a dirty sock," she says with gravitas, and then hums and nuzzles into my neck.

I'm not used to feeling this kind of happiness, especially over the holidays. The absence of my family is all too stark sometimes. But with Brin on my back, her sweet, warm breath on my cheek, my heart kicks inside my chest as I walk us to the sliding glass door and into the living room. It kicks so hard and so loud in my ears that it takes me a moment to realize we're not alone.

14

BRIN

Marco's body beneath mine goes completely still. Over his shoulder, I see a couple, man and woman, at the entryway to the apartment. They are furiously making out, starting to strip each other's clothes off.

"Ash," Marco barks out, and the man tears himself away from the woman's lips.

He's older than Marco by a few years, so mid-thirties maybe. His shirt's open so I can see the ripple of muscles that runs from neck to navel, which is completely hairless, and I don't think I've ever seen so many ab muscles in one place.

I slip off Marco's back. I don't know who this guy is, but I don't think he's supposed to be here. But then again, are we really supposed to be here either? Marco said it was fine.

Ash's eyes widen as he looks between me and Marco. There's a tense moment between the two of them until Ash breaks and turns to the woman. "Don't worry, they're leaving." He smirks at her.

"No, we're not. You are." Marco's voice is hard, unwavering.

The woman looks at us, clearly debating about who to believe.

"Let's go to your place," Ash says.

The woman turns back to Ash. "Don't you live here?"

"Yes," Ash lies. "It's fine." He runs a hand down her arm and tries to push her down the hallway. "The room at the end. I'll be in soon."

"He won't," Marco growls. "Ash, you're fired."

Ash's face morphs into an ugly sneer. "You can't fire me."

"Yes, I can—"

"Okay." The woman throws her hands up. "I'm leaving."

Ash grabs her wrist. "Hang on a second."

Marco reaches out and pushes me behind him. He prowls forward. "Let her go."

Ash lifts his hands, and the woman makes the smart decision to escape quickly. "Marco, what are you doing?" he hisses and gestures to the door. "Come on, man."

"I said you're fired. Get out of here."

"If I'm fired, I'm taking you down with me." He sneers at Marco. "You act like you're better than me but you're here doing the exact same thing." Ash gestures at me.

"Don't look at her. And don't even presume to think you know what I'm doing here. William won't even notice your departure. I'll have someone else picked out by the time he returns. He doesn't give two shits about you."

"You can't replace me!"

"I'll find out how you got into the building off schedule and I'll make sure whoever is responsible is fired too. And I'll check the security footage with a fine-toothed comb and if this isn't the first time you've abused your access to William's apartment, you'll be sure to hear about it from me."

"Fuck you!" Ash shouts. "You're just William's little pet." He grabs the nearest thing—a vase—and smashes it.

"Congratulations on your tantrum." Marco's voice is cold. "Now you have two seconds to get out the door before I call the police, which means I'll also have to call William while he's on vacation. We don't want that, do we?"

"You're such a fucking asshole, you know that?" Ash spits, but then, thank god, he leaves.

The apartment is eerily silent. Marco's breathing hard, his back to me, and I think of all the effort Marco puts into working for William. And Ash's parting words.

"You know you're not an asshole, right?"

Marco laughs, but it's dry and humorless. "You just watched me fire the personal trainer who's worked with William for years, longer than I have. I also threatened the security team of the building and probably scared that woman he was with. Ash told lies, but that wasn't one of them."

"I know you better," I say. "You're not an asshole."

Finally Marco turns to face me. "Don't you think Joe knew me better?" His voice rises. "One of the last things Joe told me was that I was an asshole, and you know what? I believe him. I am an asshole. It's literally my job."

The implication is there: *you don't know me.*

I look away from Marco. I may not know him as well as his brother did, but I don't know how to tackle this deep-seated belief that Marco has.

Instead I go looking for a dustpan. Marco bends down to pick up the big pieces of the vase and grunts at me to look in the hall closet. When I return, he's brought the trash can over and the biggest pieces have been picked up.

"Was it an expensive vase?" I ask while I sweep up the dust.

"Everything in here is expensive."

"Okay, let me rephrase the question. Will Billy Bob mourn the loss of this vase?"

Marco sighs. "No, but I liked it."

He's kneeling on the floor, holding the dustpan, so I rest the broom against the table and put both hands on his shoulders. I look right into his eyes—his weary, tired eyes. "I'm sorry for your loss."

Our faces are so close, the closest they've been since we kissed yesterday. It comes back to me in a rush, my brain having been too sleepy earlier to remember the stupid things I did yesterday.

I can't believe that we'd kissed and I'd told him I was technically a virgin. Marco is clearly LEVELS above me in that department. Just like it feels like he is dozens of steps ahead of me in life.

And how irresponsible was it of me? Marco's a good guy —despite his protestations—but I've got such a sweet deal living with him. If he thinks I'm crushing on him or we can't get back to our normal, casual roommates relationship, I'll never find another housing deal like this.

And I do *not* want to go back to multiple roommates, sketchy lease agreements, or sleeping in the living room with a curtain for privacy.

It's not worth it, even for an exceptionally good kiss.

Epically good.

I have fooled around with guys before—I'm a virgin, but I'm not *completely* inexperienced—but how is it possible that a quick makeout sesh with Marco is better than anything I've done, period?

I think Marco knows exactly what I'm thinking about because his gaze has shifted. He's looking at me with curiosity and something else . . .

I straighten, letting my hands drop and step back, looking at the apartment around us. I didn't pay attention when we came in because I was half-asleep being dragged by Marco, but holy shit, this place is amazing.

It's still decorated for Christmas, even though William isn't here. There's evergreen garland everywhere—the real stuff, not the plastic and wires of my childhood. It smells like a pine forest, and it looks a bit like one too. There are trees of multiple sizes scattered throughout the place. Everything that isn't evergreen shines: the glass ornaments, the ribbons, the candles. It's extra and over the top and I love it.

"Wow."

Marco glances up at me from the floor, where he had bent down to clean the broken vase. I walk over to the nearest tree, decorated with strings of pearls and a fine, silken golden ribbon. "Did you do all this?"

Marco snorts. "No. We hired a designer who picked everything out. I just made sure the execution went off without a hitch."

"Why is it still here?"

"William's not home, but you know how mercurial he is. He might call me up tomorrow and be over St. Barts, on his way back here. Plus the designer has events all week; they don't have time to break things down. It can wait until later. Although they did take the expensive stuff."

My eyes widen. "The expensive stuff? This isn't the expensive stuff?"

Marco comes to stand beside me and tugs on a ribbon. "The gold is gone. Anything crystal, too. Things that needed washing—linens and dishes—are gone. Probably already at some other event."

"And so, what? The trees are going to sit here, dying?"

"Yes." Marco goes back to the dustpan and sweeps the last of the ceramic dust into it. He comes to his feet and picks up the garbage can to put it back.

"Wow," I say. "Rich people."

I'm instantly fighting back bitterness. If I had a fraction of the wealth Billy Bob did, maybe I would have met Marco in a completely different situation. What if I'd had a nice apartment with responsible roommates? What if I didn't have to work outrageous hours to pay for my mistakes and had the time to date? What if Marco saw me not as someone who needed rescuing, but as a grown, confident woman, someone who he might even be attracted to?

I guess I'll never know.

15

BRIN

WHEN WE GET BACK TO OUR APARTMENT, I SHED MY COAT AND sit cross-legged on the couch, pulling up the list of activities we can do today.

Our phones ding at the same time—a Discord notice.

@everyone: Santa's elves have more work to do. There's a stack of presents waiting for every team at the hotel. Today's pile is worth six points. See you soon!

Marco comes in holding his bowl of oats and settles into the chair across from me. He's wearing a black shirt and his gray sweatpants—delicious. I wasn't awake enough to enjoy them earlier.

"I'm going to go get the presents," I announce.

Marco frowns. "Don't worry about it. I can get them after I finish eating. You should nap, you've hardly had any sleep."

"I'm fine. I could use the walk." I move to stand and Marco straightens, stopping me with a hand on my arm.

"Brin, seriously. I'll do it."

"No, don't. Relax, I'll be back before you know it." Marco can use that time to process this morning's fight with Ash.

Marco studies me for a moment, and then puts his head in his hands, his fingers gripping his hair. "I'm being an ass, aren't I?"

"Well . . . kinda. We could take a minute to breathe, you know? And I'm awake now. I think we should tackle some of the things worth more points today. Maybe something that's actually fun?" I wriggle my eyebrows at him.

He sighs and leans back in the chair. "Sure. But I'll pay for you to take an Uber to and from, that way you don't have to walk with a box of toys."

I know a good idea when I hear one so I agree. "You plan the activities for today, though, deal?"

"Deal."

———

AN HOUR LATER I'M BACK WITH A BOX OF TOYS. I'M GLAD I accepted the Uber, because yesterday's toys were twice as many as the first day, and today's toys are double that. Good thing we were getting so many points for doing this.

Marco had ordered the car for me and it waited at the hotel while I ran in. When I pull up to the curb, he's outside, ready to take the boxes upstairs.

"This is a lot," Marco grunts, putting a box of books down on our kitchen table. It's heavy, and there have probably got to be thirty books in there, mostly middle grade and YA.

I've got the box with the supplies and stuffed animals. I'm not entirely sure how we're supposed to wrap a stuffed alligator—if I was giving it as a gift I would put it in a bag.

"So." I put my hands on my hips. "Have you come up with a plan for today?"

"Yup." He turns his laptop toward me and we both bend over it looking at the spreadsheet. "I booked us tickets for ice-skating at the Rink but it's not until three, so you'll probably want to go from there right to work."

"Oh, cool," I say. "I've never been."

"To the Rink? Or Rockefeller?"

"Ice-skating."

"Oh. You never went ice-skating as a kid?"

I scrunch up my face. "Maybe once when I was really young, before my sister was born? I'm not sure." I roll my eyes. "Tennessee isn't exactly cold enough that ice-skating is a huge thing." There was an ice rink in Chattanooga during the holiday season, but it was a few hours away.

"Right, well, today I guess you'll learn how to skate."

Marco gives me a small smile, and I perk up a little. Skating sounds exciting.

"Now, until then, I was thinking we could bake cookies, and while they're in the oven or cooling, we can wrap presents."

"Okay," I agree. "What cookies should we make?"

We read the instructions: two dozen holiday-themed cookies worthy of Instagramming. We have to submit a video of the two of us eating the cookies, so presumably, we need to have two edible cookies out of the two dozen. It doesn't outright say it, but Marco and I both agree it's also an opportunity for creativity points.

We spend some time googling "cute Christmas cookies" and then debating our tactic. Marco wants to make simple sugar cookies and hand decorate. I remind him that neither of us is artistic, so I suggest these cute cookies with snowmen on top.

I win.

Marco runs out for supplies while I move the presents to the living room to give us space. I also move my big red candle over, so the room soon fills with the scent of Holiday Sparkle.

I'm six wrapped presents in when Marco returns.

He waves at me to stay where I am. "Keep working on that. I'll start on the cookies."

I get back to the wrapping, but there's a lot of banging and muttering coming from the kitchen. I hear an *oh, shit* and a lot of *hmmmm*s. Then it's a rhythmic metal-on-metal whisking.

I smile at the poinsettia wrapping paper.

"Have you ever made sugar cookies before?" I shout.

"Maybe? I can't remember. Have you?"

"Yeah, a few times."

Marco emerges, holding a bowl. He scoops up some batter with the whisk. "Does this look 'light and creamy' to you? This is just the butter and sugar. It's 'step two,' which is actually a giant paragraph that should be five steps instead."

I stand up and peer into the bowl. "No?"

"Ugh." Marco resumes beating the batter with his whisk. He's also got flour in his hair. And there's a handprint on the black T-shirt at his ribs.

"How did you get covered in flour already?"

He glances down at himself. "I'm following the recipe. Step one: whisk flour with . . . uh, stuff. I can't remember if it's baking powder or baking soda."

I raise an eyebrow. "These have to be edible cookies."

Marco scowls. "I only bought what the recipe calls for, so whichever one that was, I used it."

I hide my smile while I tape a flap of wrapping paper closed. "We don't have a mixer?"

"Nah. I didn't want to buy one for one batch of cookies. Although I guess I could have checked William's place."

"Billy Bob's," I correct, because every time I call William by the hillbilly nickname, Marco enjoys it.

He flashes a grin at me like I knew he would. "He probably has some fancy stand mixer he's never used."

"I'm pretty sure we used a stand mixer for cookies when I was growing up."

Marco harrumphs. He's whisking aggressively and my arm is getting tired just from watching him.

"I wish we had a stand mixer," I continue. "I do miss baking. I have my grandma's snowball cookie recipe somewhere." My eyes land on Marco's forearm. He's whisking nice and evenly, the whisk making circles in the batter. His muscles flex, especially where his bicep meets his forearm.

Mmm, that's nice.

He stops momentarily to shift his grip. "Let me know if you need me to take a turn," I say.

"Nah." He looks down at the bowl.

"Well, you do go to the gym, though I'm not sure what exercise you do to get strong enough for . . ." I gesture as if I'm whisking my own bowl.

I'm not entirely sure what happens, but Marco loses his grip on the bowl and the whisk flies up, spraying batter everywhere. Marco attempts to save the bowl, and his efforts work to keep the bowl from hitting the floor but not enough to save most of the batter.

Splat.

We both stare at the carpet.

"Fuck," Marco says. There's a beige blob on Bea's rug, but that's only the start of my concerns.

"Uh, do we have enough ingredients to start over?"

Marco runs a hand down his face. "No. Fuck. I'm not sure this is worth the points."

"Yeah," I say, trying to keep the disappointment out of my voice. I was looking forward to decorating.

When I look up from the floor, Marco's watching me. One corner of his lips pulls up in a slight smile. "We do have to consider, though, the enjoyment factor."

A matching smile creeps onto my face. "What, were you actually *enjoying* baking cookies?"

Marco grins at my teasing. "I was until you made the jerk-off gesture."

I gasp and shove his shoulder. "I did not!"

Now he full-on laughs and I love it. Such a change from this morning. "You totally did. You were wondering what exercise builds whisking muscles—"

"Marco!"

"Now you know." He laughs and walks away, leaving me red-faced and standing over the "light and creamy" pile of butter and sugar.

Which I now realize looks like spunk.

I get to work cleaning the floor and Marco changes clothes and then runs to the store again. This batch of batter goes much smoother and soon Marco's joining me in the living room to wrap presents.

He slumps down next to me on the ground and sighs. "Okay, two hours on the clock for the dough to chill in the fridge." He checks his watch. "We might be pushing it to get them out of the oven and decorated by the time we have to leave for ice-skating."

"We'll do our best," I tell him.

Marco digs into wrapping presents beside me and we work in silence for a while.

At least, I thought we were working in silence, until I realize I'm humming "Carol of the Bells."

I stop immediately. Marco's probably already tired of all this holiday shit. But a few minutes later, I catch myself humming again.

"Sorry," I mutter.

"We can put on music," Marco suggests.

"Sure!" I pick up my phone. "Taylor Swift okay?"

He doesn't look up. "You can put on Christmas music if you want."

I stare at him for a second and then switch to my holiday playlist before he changes his mind.

Most mornings when I wake up I have the house to myself, so it's nice to be able to play whatever music I want.

Since Thanksgiving, my preferred playlist has been my holiday one.

It's a mix of pop and orchestral pieces, so the mood goes up and down. I try to tone down my singing and dancing along but it's hard.

And then when Marco's socked toe starts wriggling in time to the music, I can't help myself anymore.

16

MARCO

BRIN STARTS BELTING OUT LYRICS, AND I DON'T REALLY MIND HER badly tuned singing. It does make the time pass faster as we wrap present after present.

She's facing away from the window, so she can't see the swirls of snow falling in the glass behind her. It's been snowing ever since I went on the second grocery run, the clouds from this morning's sunrise having fully moved in.

With the snow in the window, the flicker of Brin's candle, and the holiday music, it feels cozy inside. It makes me nostalgic, not for my childhood Christmases, but for the last Christmas I celebrated, the one where my brother was still alive and we were living with his best friend, celebrating with our friends instead of our family.

There are about thirty minutes left of chill time on the cookie and Brin is (badly) duetting with Mariah Carey when both of our phones ding.

@everyone: The city has been blessed with fresh snow this morning. It should clear up soon, so we suggest you get out there and build a snow sculpture. Send a selfie with your creation within the next hour and earn three points!

Brin and I glance at each other and then scramble up from the floor. We've got thirty minutes till the cookies need to go in the oven, half the time other teams get to build a sculpture and be as creative as possible.

We get to the park closest to us, and talk while we work to build a base. "A snowman—or woman—would be pretty straightforward. What if we dress it up as a memorable character? Like, Buddy the Elf?" Brin suggests.

"We don't have the time to get clothes together for that," I point out. "What do we have at home that we can use?"

"Umm . . . I don't know how we would get pants on it." Brin taps her chin. "What about a sundress? Oh! We could go with a full-on summer theme: sundress, sunhat, sunglasses."

"That'll work. Go grab whatever you can spare and I'll keep piling snow."

Brin runs off and returns a few minutes later when I've just started looking for branches and rocks to make the arms and face. We wrestle the dress onto the human-shaped snow, having to stop a few times to make the snow person thinner since Brin's so small.

I remember this sundress, though. It's got huge flowers on it, with capped sleeves and a skirt that flairs from the waist. Brin wears it in the summer when she takes the neighbor's kid to the park and it's sweltering.

Brin's got lean legs, strong thighs. I rarely get to see them, except when she's in this dress.

We get the dress on and Brin finishes our creation off with the hat and sunglasses. We have to press the sunglasses into its face to get them to stay and my rock smile looks unhinged, but it works. We crowd into the selfie together.

"Do they have a name?" I ask while I send the picture.

Brin studies our cheery, Frankensteined monster. "Shelley."

I sputter. "As in Mary Shelley? Like Frankenstein?"

"Yeah. Or it could be short for Sheldon. I'm not going to force our snow person into binary gender norms."

"I was literally just thinking about Frankenstein's monster too."

"Really?" She flashes me a huge grin and holds her hand up for a high five. "Great minds think alike."

"And so do ours." I smack her hand with mine while she cackles. Then I pull out my phone and we pose for a picture.

Brin puts her hands on her hips. "I do want this dress back, but it feels rude to strip it off our snow monster."

Rude or not, we do it. Then we hustle back to the apartment to roll out the dough. We don't have a rolling pin, so we use an empty wine bottle. While the cookies are in the oven, we make hot chocolate (one point) and finish wrapping the day's presents (four points).

We pull the cookies out of the oven right before we race off to Rockefeller Plaza, so we haven't decorated them yet. We'll have to do it tomorrow.

I lace my skates up and then offer Brin my hand while she gets to her feet.

"Okay," she says, once she's standing. "One goal achieved: stand on skates. That's all I actually have to do, right? Stand long enough for a picture?"

"On the ice," I clarify. "You can do this."

She's wobbly on her first step, so I offer her my arm. She takes it lightly, and we shuffle to the edge of the rink and step down onto the ice.

"Whoa!" Brin grips my arm tighter. Her knees knock together and her skates angle out. I quickly steer us out of the flow of skaters and into the middle of the rink by putting my hands on her hips and pushing.

Once we skid to a stop—I have to brake for both of us—I

bend over and lift her pant leg up. She's dressed for her shift at the restaurant, so she's in black stretchy slacks that cover the top of the skates.

"They're too loose," I tell her. "They need to feel solid on your feet, no wiggle room." I get to my knees on the hard ice in front of her and unlace her right foot.

Brin's hands fall to my shoulders as I work, bracing herself against me. I tie the second laces tighter and get to my feet.

"Better. Okay, here's what you do." I show her how to push off with one foot and we make it a few wobbly paces while she gets a feel for it. I drift alongside her, keeping my eyes on her and our fellow skaters.

I have to dodge a young kid, so I turn and skate backward right in front of Brin.

"Whoa," she says, tottering, distracted. "How did you get to be such a good skater?"

"Played a bit of hockey as a kid." That's all I offer, but Brin's never minded me being tight-lipped about my childhood. "Are you ready for us to get a picture?"

"Yeah." I let go of Brin's hand to glide toward the nearest spectator. I slowly rub my thumb over the inside of my hand.

It felt nice, holding Brin's hand. Better than nice. Super innocent and sweet and addictive.

That's something I haven't felt in a long time. I'm more of the hookup type, quick to fuck, open with my friends and prospective partners.

I am not ashamed of my sexuality or my history, but it puts it into stark relief how different we are.

I shake it off as I skid to a stop in front of the guy, who agrees to take our picture. I skate back to Brin and we pose, smiling.

"Thank you so much," Brin says to the man as she shuffles her way to me as I take my phone back. We join the flow of traffic and I check the pictures.

"Uh."

Brin looks at me. "What is it?"

I swipe. And swipe again. He took three pictures of us: one before we posed, so I'm still moving and blurry; one with Brin's eyes closed; and one where he pulled the phone away as he was pressing the shutter so everything's blurry.

I show Brin the pictures and she blanches. "Ew. I look like I'm high. Do you think that will get us creativity points? Skating while under the influence?"

"Maybe negative points. Let's try again."

She lifts her chin toward a guy standing at the edge of the rink looking at his phone. "We can ask him."

I draw my brows together, confused. "Why him?"

"His daughter is skating over there." She nods toward a young teen spinning in circles near the center. "She skated over a while ago and he helped fix her hair and gave her a snack. He's got airport dad vibes. Why don't we ask for a video, then all he has to do is point it in the right direction."

I make my way over to the guy. "Excuse me?" He looks up. "Would you mind taking a quick video of us?"

"Sure."

Two minutes later we have a halfway decent video of me skating back to Brin and then the two of us waving at the camera.

"Thanks so much, I appreciate it."

"Yeah, thanks!" Brin's caught up to us and offers Airport Dad a warm smile.

"No problem," he says. "Great date idea." He gives me a nod, like "you've done well," and Brin laughs.

I take her hand and skate us away from him. We're quiet for a moment and then Brin says, "Have you ever taken anyone skating on a date before?"

I think for a minute. "No? Not that I recall."

"You should," she says. After a beat, she continues. "It's

very . . ." She waves her free hand in my direction. "Competence porn, watching you skate."

I snort.

"You should take a date skating," she repeats, but almost like she's talking to herself. "I've never even heard you mention having a date."

"Pot. Kettle." I gesture between us.

She laughs. "It's just surprising, because . . . you know." She gestures at me with a "duh" tone.

"I'm not going to bring someone home to the room we share." I return her tone.

She rolls her eyes. "Obviously. But, like, what's your type?"

I think about my answer. *Redheads that barely come up to my chin. Five-foot-something balls of energy. Someone who is too nice to be with an asshole like me.*

That's not an answer that I can give, so I go with some honest history. Brin already knows I'm bisexual, but she doesn't know how widely my tastes range. "My first crush was confusing because it was *both* the boy's locker room bully and his cheerleader girlfriend. And then my best friend, a nerdy gamer. Then a drag queen—both in and out of drag. Pretty much any type of queer man for a while, because that's who I hung out with the most. The last person I slept with was a woman, a model I met at one of William's parties."

"Billy Bob," she says absentmindedly.

"What about you?" I ask. "What's your type?"

A dark look passes over her face, but then she yawns.

"That"—I point at her—"is a problem. I *knew* you needed a nap."

"I'm fine," she insists. But she also doesn't argue when I steer us both toward the exit.

We heel-toe to the bench seats and Brin sits down hard. "We'll get you some caffeine," I say as she yawns again. I get down on my knees and unlace her boots for her.

"I'll be fine once I get to work."

"Let's hope so," I mutter.

17

BRIN

The amount of trust Marco has in me must be exorbitant, because he places my ice skate between his legs while he unlaces it. Any man that's okay putting an eight-or-so-inch blade that close to his junk is brave.

Stepping onto the ice had been a little scary, but Marco oozes confidence and the way he matter-of-factly goes about things is addictive. I had joked about that dad watching the girl skate being an airport dad, but honestly, Marco gives me those vibes too.

Like how he held my hand while we skated, using it to carefully steer me or provide me support. And now, he's kneeling on the floor, having not even taken off his own skates yet, and is putting my feet back into my unsexy black work sneakers.

It's so hard for him to see himself as not an asshole, but I see it every day.

Done, he pivots to sit next to me on the bench, swapping his skates out while I wait. I have to admit, I am tired. Staying up late last night and then getting up so early to watch the sunrise has taken a toll on me.

"Marco? Wait, Brie?"

The voice jolts me upright, and the name—a nickname I only used on Sugary—makes my stomach sink like lead.

"Wow, I did not recognize you the other day." Greg sits down next to Marco, ice skates in hand, but his eyes are on me.

Marco glances at me. "You two have met?"

Greg smiles, warm eyes twinkling. *The devil in disguise.* "You could say that. Went on a couple dates. You went by Brie on the app, though, right?"

My stomach dips. He could be talking about any app but he's specifically not mentioning the name. Does he not want Marco to know he was on Sugary?

"Right," I say, looking away and down to adjust the tongue of my sneakers.

Marco turns to Greg, and I don't know if he does it to divert Greg's attention away from me, but he asks how the scavenger hunt is going for his team.

"Good." Greg says it smugly. "I won't tell you how many points we have, because I don't want you thinking there's any hope for you to win our bet. We've been going hard for the creativity points, so it'll all boil down to the judges' scoring."

I'm relieved to have Greg's attention off me. I'm fine with letting the guys have their own little contest as long as I don't have to be involved. If we win, I'll have to figure out a way to not be around when Greg is playing Marco's errand boy.

If we lose, though . . . maybe I'll never have to see Greg again. I don't think Marco and I have done well on our creativity points. We've mostly been trying to cross off as many items as we can. I mean, it's hard to skate creatively when you've never skated before, but I'm getting worried. We're already constrained by my work schedule, and the clock is ticking.

"We'll see," Marco says. He then stands, grabbing my hand to pull him up with me. "We've got to get going. Have fun skating."

They fist-bump and Marco guides me out of the area, his hand on the small of my back. When we're clear of the crowd and headed toward the subway, Marco leans in. "You dated?"

"A while ago, and it was one date. It's not a big deal."

Marco drops it and we get in line for coffee.

Why *didn't* I say anything to him before? Because I am embarrassed by the whole Sugary thing? Or is it because Marco likes Greg, and I don't want to risk him not believing me?

Or do I just want it all to go away? To not upset anyone and ignore the problem? Classic fawning move.

Great, now I'm psychoanalyzing myself.

The Sugary thing *is* embarrassing. Signing up for a "luxury dating app" that is actually full of women looking for a sugar daddy and men who are willing to "spoil" their dates is not something Brin two years ago would have done. My parents definitely would have had a lot of nasty things to say about me signing up for it, but I'm working really hard to not let them make me feel bad anymore.

When Marco had asked me what my type was, the first thing that came to mind was how much Greg and Marco are alike—tall, dark hair, lean and fit bodies, an affinity for suits, and an aura of Men Who Get Shit Done. Handsome.

The difference being that Marco operates under the false impression that he is a bad person.

Whereas Greg truly is the devil in disguise.

———

My shift sucks. I'm running on fumes most of the night, and a few tables notice. My tips aren't as great as the night before and I drop an entire tray of drinks. At least it wasn't an arancini-in-the-purse situation again.

Plus, I checked my phone on break and I totally missed a burst challenge. It was only a one-pointer, but still. Marco and I could have totally found a dreidel and learned how to play.

I'm supposed to be full of holiday cheer right now, and instead I'm dead on my feet, behind the bar with Eva, counting up my tips and transferring my open tabs.

Which is why I think I'm dreaming when I see Marco take a seat at the bar. He's hung his jacket on the back of his stool and he's wearing . . .

An ugly Christmas sweater.

Unlike the "ugly" ones (not so much ugly as tacky) we'd looked at together when we'd first seen it on the list, this sweater is really, truly hideous. It looks like it was hand-crocheted, and whoever planned this atrocity didn't understand how perspectives worked. The reindeer on the front has mismatched eyes and one of its legs is bent in a way that's more likely to get it put down than successfully flying a sleigh. And the colors in the borders of the design are truly disturbing—the green is fine, but the red is actually hot pink, and there's white speckles on the shoulders, which are maybe supposed to be snow but make it look like Marco has dandruff.

Eva is cackling. "Oh my god. I am DYING."

"What are you wearing?" I ask, incredulous.

Guiltily, Marco reaches down to a bag at his feet and pulls out another ugly sweater. This one is mostly black, but with an enormous Santa head on the front, complete with a hat and a giant beard, which actually dangles down past the hem. It's like a flap on the front of the sweater. But the worst part is that Santa looks sad. He has two beady eyes and his beard parts to expose a thin mouth that's either designed to be frowning or has sagged as it's been worn.

"Sorry." Marco's face doesn't look sorry. "This one's too small for me."

"Just when you thought they couldn't get any uglier,

huh?" Eva cracks. "Now come on, put it on so I can get a picture."

I gingerly pull the sweater over my head. It at least smells clean.

Eva cackles as she takes our picture. She hands Marco his phone, and we strip the sweaters off. "Okay, before you go home, though, I've got to tell you this story. You won't believe what I heard today."

Marco sips his soda, amused. I blink and push back a strand of hair, trying to pay attention to my friend. "What?"

"Austin's getting married."

"Wait. I know Theo's getting married—" Theo is one of the servers, and he plans to propose to his girlfriend over Christmas. We're all ninety-nine percent sure she's going to say yes, since they have two kids together and she's been telling him he doesn't get any more until he puts a ring on it. "But who's Austin?"

"I met him on the app last year. We dated a few times. He took me to the Knicks game. Ringing any bells?"

"Vaguely," I admit.

She explains to Marco that she'd gone on five dates with the guy, he'd been generous (which is saying a lot, given the nature of Sugary), and he'd been a bit of a romantic. Their dates had fizzled, at least on Eva's side. And now, apparently, he's engaged to the woman he met right after her.

I rub my temples. "Did you want to marry him?"

"Not really," she admits. "But I was thinking about how Terry is also engaged now. And Zach. That's three that I know about, and you know what they say, twice a coincidence, three times a trend."

"So what are you saying?" Marco asks.

"Well, maybe my vagina's magical."

Marco snorts up some of his Diet Coke.

"You've slept with all these guys?" I ask.

Eva looks at me, and I quickly add, "Not in judgment. More of . . . awe? Assuming it was good, I mean."

She shrugs. "Meh."

Well, that sums that up. I hope that when I finally do it, I get more than mediocre sex. I try not to look at Marco when I have this thought. Because if the kiss was anything to go by, Marco does not have meh sex.

"It's a theory," she says. "I might have to experiment."

"How would you . . ." Marco shakes his head. "Never mind. This conversation could take forever. I want to get Brin home."

Eva waves me out of the bar. "By all means, go home. You're dead on your feet, girlie."

"What are you even doing here anyway?" I ask Marco as we walk to the front door. "We could have done the sweaters at home."

"I figured maybe we'd get a few creativity points for actually wearing them in public. Plus I wanted to make sure you got home safe." He takes my coat from me and holds it out so I can put it on. Just before we walk out the door, I stop and run back and pull Eva into a hug.

"Since you're not working Tuesday, I won't see you until Christmas," I say. Mondays are my normal day off, I work on Tuesday, and then the restaurant is closed for the twenty-fourth and twenty-fifth.

"What—awe." She hugs me back, hard.

"Merry Christmas," I say, and she says it back before shoving me out the door.

18

BRIN

It's the last day of the scavenger hunt, and coincidentally also the last day of Hanukkah. When I get up in the morning, there are no presents to wrap, which is a blessing because after yesterday, we have three paper cuts between the two of us and I hope I never have to see another roll of wrapping paper in my life.

We finish decorating the cookies. Our first problem is that we rolled the dough out really unevenly, so some of them are half-burnt. We use icing to flood the cookie, making it look like a snowman has melted, before sticking a large marshmallow on top, which we give a face using black thick icing.

Getting icing to the right consistency is hard—some of our melted snowman icing is too thin and the cookies are barely covered. Some of the black icing is too thick to make fine dots for the faces, and they turn out more like the mask from the movie *Scream*.

But whatever. We position the best ones up front for the photo and then take a video of us eating them. Two more points on the scoreboard, even though our snowman cookies don't look as good as the photos we found online.

With the leftover marshmallows, we play chubby bunny,

which I haven't played since my high school days. I get ten marshmallows in my mouth while still intelligibly saying "cubby bunny" but then I have to stop because I'm laughing too hard. Mostly I'm laughing because Marco is straight up *cackling,* and weirdly has never heard of the game before. And damn him, even with his cheeks stuffed, he's still ridiculously sexy.

Afterward, I have a sugar rush from consuming more marshmallows than I put on cookies.

Marco and I pull on our coats and head out. Our next goal is to get a picture with the world's largest menorah at Grand Army Plaza. We get that sent in and then head to Prospect Park for another task—create a nature mandala.

On the way, we research what a mandala actually is. "'A geometric design that represents the universe,'" Marco reads. His brows draw together in confusion and then he shakes his head. "Image results," he mutters.

I peer over his shoulder as we scroll through the images.

"Oh. I see. Those are cool. We need to gather supplies."

When we get to the park, I scour the ground while Marco reads out loud to me about mandalas. They're supposed to be meditative, and are often used to honor the solstice. Soon, Marco puts his phone away and helps me make neat piles of pine cones, needles, sticks, rocks, whatever we can find.

My stomach is starting to grumble, but I do my best to ignore it. This is meditative, my hunger can wait.

We make the first ring of the mandala, alternating pine needle bundles and long pine cones. It's like building a snowflake.

We're halfway to the second layer when both our phones ding.

@everyone: The next burst challenge is here! Celebrate the last day of Hanukkah by eating some sufganiyot. Take a picture of <u>both team members</u> with one in the next ten

minutes and upload it for two points. Note: to accommo-
date those with dietary restrictions, the sufganiyot does
not have to be consumed . . . but if you are able, why not
enjoy a Jewish baked treat while you can?

I google sufganiyot and the picture of a jelly-filled donut
pops up.

"Oh my god, can we *please* go eat one?" My stomach
grumbles as if it knows sugar and fat are headed its way. "We
can come back to the mandala."

Marco smiles and dusts off his hands. "Sure. We're in a
good place for it too. Plenty of options in Brooklyn."

We do some quick searching, find a bakery, and head
toward Washington Avenue. I jog to keep up with Marco's
long strides, because the bakery is a few minutes away and
who knows if there will be a line. We might have to take a
picture with the display first before waiting in line.

"God, my stomach is so excited."

"Yeah, I'm hungry too."

"What, is your oatmeal not keeping you satisfied?" I tease.
The light changes and I step off the curb at the intersection to
cross.

"Normally it—Brin!"

Tires squeal and I'm jerked off my feet. Everything goes
black as my face is buried in something soft.

19

MARCO

I catch Brin's wrist and yank her to me, barely saving her from being struck and pulling us back onto the sidewalk. The car honks while it flies past, but I barely hear it.

That was close. Too close.

I wrap my arms around Brin and hold her tight, her face buried into my chest. I close my eyes and press my lips to the top of her head.

It wasn't like this with my brother. I'd been too far away to pull him out of the path of the oncoming car. I'd been too far away to do anything, trapped watching the moment that stretched on never ending and simultaneously took less than a heartbeat to change my world.

What if that had happened to Brin? What if I hadn't been able to get a grip on her in time?

What if all we'd had between us was a single glorious kiss?

I've often thought about what life would have been like if Joe hadn't died. I have dreams where I get to tell him I love him again, where I can hug him. Things that I didn't do enough during his life.

Brin stirs against me, and I realize she's talking. It's slow and soft, soothing words to calm me.

I'm shaking.

Her arms encircle my waist, her hand gently strokes my back.

We stand like that for minutes, hours, forever. Long enough that the hug shifts, and changes, and starts to feel good in a different way.

"Brin," I croak. I clear my throat and try again. "Brin."

She pulls her face out from the armpit of my coat and looks up at me. Her hairband's askew and her hair sticks up in weird places, but those sky-blue eyes gaze up at me in concern.

I hold her gaze while I lower my mouth slowly, carefully, to hers. I love the way her eyelashes flutter and the way her lips part. I love that she's comforting me. I love the way she fits in my arms.

I *love* her.

And I have to tell her. I can hear Joe in my head telling me that love should not be denied, no matter what the world says or the risks you take.

So I press my mouth to hers. Brin's gasp gives me an opening and I take it, sweeping into her mouth and deepening our kiss. She groans, and while we've been pressed together ever since I pulled her from the oncoming traffic, it's entirely different now. I feel lit up from my head to my toes.

Brin's hands tighten when I pull back. "Don't say this is a bad idea," she pleads. "I know it is. But I really, really don't want to stop this time."

I take a deep breath and let out a shaky exhale. "I don't want to stop either."

Brin grins at me. "Thank god."

Then her lips are on mine again, and they're deep, long kisses. Brin reaches up on her tiptoes, and I bend my knees to meet her. She feels tiny in my arms, a little slip I can curl around and protect.

But . . . it's not exactly comfortable the longer we make out, so when we next come up for air, I suggest going home. Brin nods and I hail a taxi.

In the backseat I pull her into me. My fingers cup the back of her neck and I use my thumb to tilt her face to me. I sip from her mouth, slow, aching kisses.

The driver has to interrupt us to tell us that we're home. I pay as Brin hops out and waits for me at the door to our place.

I'm overwhelmed by the urge to do this right. If Brin wants to take this slow, I'll be the most patient man in the world. I'll show her that sex doesn't mean penetration, that I can blow her fucking mind with everything I have.

And if she does want to go all the way . . . I'll make it so fucking good.

I get that first times *shouldn't* be that big of a deal, but they still can be, and Brin's waited all this time.

No matter what she wants, I'm going to pour all of my love into whatever she's willing to give me.

20

BRIN

WHEN WE RETURN TO THE APARTMENT, WE HARDLY GET INSIDE the door and take our shoes and coats off before Marco is on me again, his fingers twisting into my hair and his mouth hot on mine. Now that we're in the privacy of our own home, I can do whatever I want. A small part of my brain says that this is Marco—my roommate and one of my best friends. Am I sure this is what I want?

The rest of my brain—and my body—really want to do more. And I know Marco wants me to be comfortable, to set the pace. That means I take us the next step forward, hovering my hand over his lap. "Is this okay?" I ask, nerves fluttering in my stomach.

"Very okay."

I grip his erection through his jeans. Marco groans and pulls his mouth away from mine. He sits down on the couch and pulls me into the cradle of his thighs. "If you want to take it slow," he says, "I'll be careful with you, okay?"

"I know you will." I nod my head as much as I can in his hold. "I know you think you're an asshole, but I think it's everyone else who's an asshole. I've only ever seen this tender, kind man." I kiss him this time, lips firm before I pull back. "Also, let me be clear. You're incredibly sexy."

This grin he gives me is wolfish, and he reaches out, using his other hand to pull me into his lap where I straddle him. "Me? You're the one who's made me *hard* so much. You have no idea."

In between kisses, we tell each other hot little secrets we've kept.

"I like it when you come back from a run in the summer and you take off your shirt and sweat drips down your chest." I run my hand down his pecs, feeling the way his breath comes faster.

Marco nips my lip. "Now that I know what your vibrator looks like I've had some hardcore fantasies about it."

My hands make it down to his abs. "Your gray sweatpants are obscene."

He chuckles, and tilts my head to the side, trailing kisses down my neck. Beneath me, he shifts, turning us slightly. "I heard you orgasm in the shower the other day."

My breath hitches when he hits a particularly sensitive spot, and he falls back against the couch, pulling me along with him. Face-to-face, I meet Marco's gaze. "I was thinking about you."

We're lying on the couch now, Marco beneath me. I can feel how much Marco enjoys that last little secret by the way his rock-hard dick twitches against my thigh. He groans and thrusts his tongue inside my mouth.

God, kissing him feels so good. If kissing him is this good . . .

When I pull back, his gaze is hooded, lusty. My insides are tangled in knots and all I want is the exact right tug to unravel them. "How far are we going to go?" I ask, my voice hoarse.

I feel it all over when Marco groans. "You're asking me?" His hands knead my upper thighs. "You're the one who shouldn't rush. Virginity is a bullshit concept, but it doesn't mean you don't have complicated feelings about it." He lets go of my ass. One hand moves behind his head, making his bicep bulge. The other rests on my waist and he gently asks, "Do you want to talk about why you haven't done it before?"

I prop my head up on my fist so I can look down at Marco. His hand on my waist starts making small circles. "Well, first of all, I was taught abstinence in school and at church." I punch the air with my free hand. "Yay, Catholicism. My parents also made me wear a purity ring and . . ." I shrug. "It wasn't until I moved here that I was disabused of the idea that sex hurts." My cheeks are flushed, giving away my embarrassment. Eva has enthusiastically encouraged me, and I definitely wouldn't be on top of Marco right now if she didn't treat sex like it was something to be celebrated and enjoyed.

"It definitely will not hurt," Marco says firmly.

"I know. I mean, you've seen my vibrator. I've . . . done it with that, and you know I use tampons, so it's not like my hymen's intact."

Marco's eyes close and he makes a pained expression.

I bite my lip. "Too much information?"

"No, I'm picturing you with the toy."

I laugh and bend down to kiss him again. I've been exploring Marco's body, anything I can get my hands on. My palms fit so right curled around his shoulders. When I drag them up his neck and into his hair I can tangle my fingers in his dark locks and hold him tighter.

"Is this okay?" I whisper.

Instead of continuing, Marco pulls back to look up at me. "I think you keep asking me if things are okay because some-where deep inside you thinks that none of this is okay. That's the purity culture talking, Brin. I promise everything *is* going to be okay. I will take care of you and I will make this good for you . . . if you want to keep going?"

"I do, I do," I say quickly. "You're right. It's this nagging voice, but it's not real. I want this."

Marco bends his head and breathes one word onto my skin. "Good." He's holding on to the backs of my thighs, right where they meet my ass. His fingers trace a slow, lazy line across my pants, and I squirm against him. "This is real," he says. "How much I want to pleasure you is very real."

I shudder and, emboldened, I roll slightly over to my side and reach my free hand down to grab Marco through his pants.

His eyes fly open and he grabs me, letting his fingers curl around my wrist. "Stop that," he pants. "There's only so much I can take before I'm going to make a mess."

I flush even harder, flattered that he thinks I could make him cum in his pants.

He drags my hand away, yet still arches up to rub against me the best he can. I meet his hips with mine and then we're making out again.

Friction against Marco feels so good. The fly of his jeans sits right against my clit and Marco lets me take the lead, rubbing myself over and over again against him. We're not even making out anymore; I'm panting too hard and Marco's pressed his head back into the arm of the couch, the muscles of his neck straining and his eyes squeezed shut.

His Adam's apple is right in front of me, and I lick it.

It bobs when he laughs, a pained noise. "Fuck, Brin."

"I've wanted to do that for so long."

He opens his eyes and looks at me. "Yeah? How long?"

"Probably fourteen-ish months."

He laughs. "Since we moved in together?"

I nod. I'm still twisting my hips, rubbing against his straining erection. "How about you? Is there anything you've wanted to do to me?"

Marco's eyes flash. "Everything."

"Come on," I tease, and nibble on his neck. "One specific thing."

"Well, I definitely want to watch you use that toy. Maybe even on me."

I shudder. Wow. I did not know that it would turn me on so much to think about that.

"Brin? Is that something you'd like?"

I realize I've stopped moving. "Yeah," I say. "But right now, I just . . ." I move my hips against him again.

His voice gets deeper. "What do you need? What do you want?"

I bite my lip and look up at him. "I really want to keep going."

I have a moment of doubt—I know that's not specific, and it's probably not what Marco was looking for, but he accepts it anyway.

Effortlessly, Marco wraps his arms around me and stands up from the couch. I let out an "eep," which makes him laugh. "Oh is this what it's like way up here?"

He presses a hard kiss to my mouth while walking us into our bedroom.

The room spins as I fall backward onto the bed. Marco shucks off his jeans, leaving his boxer-briefs on.

Hello thighs.

He runs his hands up my legs and hooks his fingers into my yoga pants, waiting for permission. I nod and he peels them off my legs. I'm not wearing any underwear beneath, so the cool air hits me right where I'm flushed and hot from rubbing against Marco.

Marco kneels on the bed and helps me shed my shirt and bra. Then he picks my foot up and brings it to his mouth. He squeezes hard and then softly runs his lips over the arch of my foot, tickling me. I try to kick out and can barely move.

I scream, laughing, and then Marco's smile is on the soft spot below my ankle bone. He makes his way up my leg, presses kisses and licks along the way. Halfway up, I can barely stand it, and tell him so.

He ignores me, and keeps moving at that slow, sedated pace. It's hard not to tense up in anticipation as he draws closer and closer to my center.

Marco nips my thigh. "Breathe, or I'll take my time going up the other leg too."

"It does feel left out." I can barely get the joke out as I try to restart my labored breathing.

"Has anyone ever done this to you?" Marco asks.

"Yeah. But not very well. Or at least, not enough to figure out if I like it or not."

"Oh you'll like it."

I can barely process the words before his mouth is on me and my whole body arches. "Whoa!"

Marco chuckles and bands one of his arms around my hips and presses me into the bed. "I'm going to use my fingers, too. If I do anything you don't like, tell me, okay?" I nod. "And for fuck's sake, tell me if I do something that feels really good."

"I will. Marco, please." I am so wound up it hurts.

"I know, gorgeous," he soothes. And then I watch as he sucks a finger into his mouth and moistens it. My legs curl around his head when he presses it into me, and then his mouth returns to my clit with a long swipe of his tongue.

I can't tell exactly what Marco's doing, but whatever it is it's amazing. I let my head fall back and close my eyes. There's the stretch and pull of what I'm pretty sure is multiple fingers inside of me now, and the steady sucking of his lips on my clit is bringing me higher and higher.

"More, harder, oh god." I don't even really know what I'm asking of him.

Marco does everything more and harder. Pressure inside me is building up and I lift my head to look at him. When we make eye contact, he lets out a groan that I feel all the way through my core.

My hands are in his hair, gripping his head as if to prevent him from going anywhere. My thighs are in on it too—they're clamped tight on his ears.

I can feel his shoulder moving as his fingers pump in and out of me and my whole body tenses in one breaking glorious wave as I come hard on his tongue—harder than I've ever come in my life, harder than I knew was possible.

Marco's eyes close, and I do the same, letting my head fall back, rocking against Marco's hand as my orgasm hits me over and over again.

Then it's over, leaving me faster than it came on, and I collapse back onto the bed. Marco slows, his eyes meeting mine and glinting as he slowly licks and massages me. It feels dreamy, the way he lets his fingers slide over my slick lips.

My legs fall open, relaxed now, and Marco lays his head on my thigh, still stroking me.

Everything I've experienced up until this point was amateur hour. I am relieved I never had intercourse with anyone else I fooled around with. I want Marco to be the first.

21

MARCO

LIFE STILLS INSIDE THE APARTMENT. BRIN GIVES A SOFT HUM. HER body is loose and languid underneath me, and I keep gently playing with her pussy. I'm careful not to touch her clit and to keep things light until she's ready for more.

I'm ignoring my aching dick. Everything about Brin is driving me wild: her smell, her taste, the light thatch of hairs between her legs, her moans, the way her body clamped down on my fingers when she was coming.

There's a wet spot underneath her and my fingers are absolutely soaked. It's so fucking hot.

Finally Brin stirs. She may have been half-asleep, because the way she says my name reminds me of our early morning watching the sunrise.

I kiss her thigh before crawling up her body so we're face-to-face.

Her eyes barely open when she smiles at me. "I want it like this."

"Yeah?" I whisper, kissing her jaw, the side of her neck.

"Please."

I stand up and strip my clothes off. I have condoms under my bed and I fish one out, praying it's not expired.

Whew, next year. I slide the condom on and look down at my dick.

Okay, I think at it. *This is a time to be slow and steady and not blow my load right out of the gate. Her first time shouldn't be over in ten seconds.*

I have concerns about my ability to perform because it feels like I've had Brin rubbing up on me for hours and the smell and taste of her inside me for almost as long. But when my already-sex-blissed virgin roommate tells me she wants me, by god I'm going to deliver the best I can.

Climbing back on the bed, I crawl up to Brin. "Just so you know," I say. "I'm on PrEP and I've been tested since the last time I was with someone."

Brin looks up at me, a bit more awake now. She reaches up and traces the line of my jaw with a delicate touch. "I've got an IUD. And I haven't done this before, but I've done other stuff." Her eyes skitter away. "I probably should have gotten tested at some point, but it's, uh, been a long time. Sorry."

I move my head to meet her gaze. "Don't apologize." I kiss her quickly and line myself up. I have to curl my back to keep my head next to hers to watch her as I press inside. At first she stills, but then her eyelashes flutter and her breath quickens. She hums in pleasure, and I stroke a few times, easing my way in until I bottom out.

Beneath me, Brin's quiet. We're gazing at each other while we catch our breaths.

"Does it feel okay?" I ask her.

"Yeah." She shifts, and I hold my breath while her body tightens around me.

My elbows are on either side of her shoulders, propping myself up. "No pain?"

She shakes her head. "Full. You're . . . ah . . . a little bigger than my vibrator."

"I don't have as many functions, sorry to disappoint."

She laughs and my breath hitches.

"It feels more different than I thought it would. My vibrator is supposed to be lifelike, but it's really not." She says it with wonder in her voice.

"Better or worse?"

"Oh, definitely better. I don't know—" She gazes out over my shoulder, her eyes going unfocused. "I can't describe it." She arches her back, wriggling against me, and I groan. Then she lifts her knees up and circles her legs around my waist and I press in even deeper. "Oh," she says. "Do that again."

I brace myself and rock gently. Her eyelashes flutter and I do it again and again.

Brin grabs on to my biceps, her fingers digging into the muscles. "More," she pants.

I shift so my forearms brace on the bed next to her ears, my triceps against her shoulders to give me leverage, and I thrust harder. Her breath hits my throat and my lips are on her forehead as I give her the shallow grinds against her body that make her fingernails dig in deeper and deeper.

Fuck, I don't think I'm going to make it.

I grit my teeth, dig my own fingernails into my palm, do anything I can think of to stave it off, because I want Brin to come again so badly.

Finally, I feel it first on my dick. It's a flood and a squeeze and then Brin's body curls up to mine and her head falls back on a silent scream. Then I can finally let go.

I press my lips tight as my body shudders in climax. The snap of pleasure is sharp and snatches my breath away. I can't tell if the quakes come from me or her.

Either way, when my brain comes back online, I'm still above her, my body sagging but my arms still holding most of my weight. Brin's legs have flopped to either side; her hands have let go of me and rest on the bed. I ease off carefully, pressing a kiss to Brin's lips as I disengage.

"How do you feel?" My throat is coarse, my voice coming out like gravel.

She grunts, and as soon as I'm clear enough, she turns onto her side and buries her face into the pillow.

I get up and dispose of the condom. I clean myself up, and as much as I don't want to disturb her, she's gotta get up and take care of herself too.

"Brin." I kiss her hip. "Hey. You should go pee to prevent a UTI. Come on."

I tug and murmur at her until she gets up, unsteady, and help her walk to the bathroom.

While she's doing that, I grab our phones. We haven't eaten lunch, and I'm thinking of ordering delivery. I open up my phone and there's a new notification:

@everyone: That's a wrap! Congratulations on all of your points. Thank you for participating in the first annual SHiNY Season. We hope you had a blast. See you on the 27th!

I show Brin the message when she gets back to bed.

"We didn't get either the sufganiyot or the mandala points," she pouts.

I lean over to kiss her. "We got something better."

Brin laughs. "True. I guess we'll know in a few days whether we won or not."

Our scavenger hunt is over, and I don't think I care anymore about winning. Because maybe I already won, when I have Brin naked in my arms.

22

BRIN

I'm sure married sex is amazing too—maybe? How would I know?—but I wake up feeling really good.

Marco's not in bed with me, but when I get dressed and shuffle out of our bedroom to pee, I find him on the couch with his laptop. He tells me good morning and I blink back at him and say hello in my gritty morning voice.

When I come out of the bathroom Marco's waiting for me, a little shyness in his gaze that I'm not used to seeing. It's endearing.

"How do you feel?" he asks. "Sore?"

I wind my arms around his neck and, morning breath and all, kiss him. He smiles against my lips and relaxes. When we pull apart, he asks, "Would you like breakfast in bed?"

"Ooooo, yes please."

I get back into his bed, snuggling under the blankets. A few minutes later, Marco comes in with peanut-buttered toast and coffee. I sit up, propping myself up with a giant pile of pillows, and Marco sits next to me while I eat.

"Do you have plans today?" I ask between bites.

Marco shakes his head. "I'm hoping just you."

I laugh. "Well, I do have to work, so I only have a few hours."

"Plenty of time for a short sexfest."

"Is that the official term?"

"Totally."

"How many hours is a long sexfest?" I muse.

"Well, a sexfest implies multiple orgasms by all parties, and if we have a few hours for a short sexfest then a long sexfest has to be like . . . six hours?"

I nearly choke on my toast. "Oh my god. Have you ever had a long sexfest?"

He just grins.

"Okay, well maybe we should save our energy today and have a long sexfest tomorrow, since I'm not working on Christmas Eve."

Marco's smile drops. "Actually, I'm going to go visit my brother's grave tomorrow."

"Oh my god." I sit up. "I didn't know. I'm so glad you go out to visit him. Do you want me to go with you? Oh wait, I have to babysit tomorrow. That puts a damper on our long sexfest too. When will you go to the cemetery?"

"Don't worry about it," he says quickly, and I study his face to make sure he really is okay with going alone. "Joe didn't have a will, so my parents did whatever they wanted and he's out in Long Island. Which is why I have a will because I do *not* want to end up at the whim of my parents."

Wow. He has a will. That's boss-level adulting.

"That must have been a tough time for you. Joe's funeral and dealing with your parents and not being able to carry out Joe's wishes."

"It was. The shittiest thing was that my parents thought I'd have a relationship with them again. Like I'd forget their cruelty and now that Joe was gone everything would be fine."

I cocked my head. "They'd accept your bisexuality but not Joe being gay?"

Marco grins wickedly. "They don't know. I want them to know that I'm rejecting them, not the other way around."

That delights me. I finish the last of my toast and take a few sips of my still-cooling coffee.

Marco clears his throat. "Regarding said sexfest: Is there anything you want to do?"

"Like . . . ?"

He counts off with his fingers. "Positions. Acts. I'm sure we can find a sex shop that's open today and pick up any supplies."

"Huh. I haven't really thought about it."

Marco tilts his head at me. "What do you think about when you're using the dildo?"

I blush. "Oh, um, well . . . you already know I think about you . . ."

He grins, showing all his teeth. "Yeah? You think about me doing what?"

Oh my god. Why is it so hard to say naughty things? "In the shower," I finally say.

He pulls out his phone and I watch over his shoulder as he starts a note. *Shower sex,* he types. Then he adds, *watch Brin use her toy* and then *use toy on Brin.*

He glances up at me. "Mind if I make some suggestions?"

I gesture with my mug. "By all means."

Reverse cowgirl.

Okay, that one I know.

Doggy style.

Yup, heard of that one too.

Prone bone.

"What the hell is that one?" I blurt.

"Oh, I'll show you. Now hurry up and finish your coffee, gorgeous."

————

By the time I'd finished my coffee the list was about thirty items long—a lot to tackle in a short sexfest, but Marco's trying his best.

He starts by tugging on my ankles, pulling me down to lie on my back, and peeling the pajamas off my legs. Then he dives in, face-first, and brings me to a quick climax with his mouth.

Then he flips me over and crawls on top of me. I still have my shirt on, but Marco rucks it up and presses his whole body against mine, kissing the back of my neck. He's gotten undressed, probably while I was in a post-orgasm fugue state, and so our bodies are skin to skin.

His weight pressing me down is so sexy it sends a shiver up my spine. His lips trace a path up to my ear, and he nibbles on my earlobe. "I'm gonna get a condom, okay? Then I'm going to show you the wonders of the prone bone. I think you'll like it."

I hear the nightstand drawer open, and the rip of the foil. Then Marco's back, straddling my thighs. "Lift up a bit, gorgeous." He taps my hip so I know what he means. When I spread my legs, he tells me to close them.

He enters me slowly until he's bottomed out and then pushes me down to lie flat. His hands grip my ass, spreading my cheeks slightly. Oh god, what can he see?

"Fuck that's hot. Look at you taking me so well."

My butt checks clench in his hand as my body tightens at the compliment. He chuckles and then lies down over me.

It's more intimate than I was expecting for a position from behind. Marco holds himself over me so he doesn't smother me, and that gives him room to pepper me with kisses anywhere he can reach. His strokes are smooth and steady, and on my stomach like this I can clench my muscles. My orgasm builds, deeper this time, and soon he's grunting in my ear, his hips steadily rocking us both to the peak.

I cry out, clenching around him, and Marco follows with a deep thrust and a guttural groan.

We lie in silence, catching our breaths. When Marco finally rolls off, I turn my head to look at him.

God he's gorgeous. His body is coated in a slight sheen of sweat—he did all the work—and I'm eye level with his ribs. I raise my head a little and get an amazing view of his V all the way down to his soft dick.

Marco rubs his face and checks his phone for the time. "Do you think you can come again?"

"Can *you*?" I mean, Marco's thirty-two and what they hell do I know, but I didn't think men could get hard again that fast.

"I have something else in mind. Stay there."

I obey. I watch him as much as I can though, turning my head while he opens my sock drawer. Even before he pulls out the hot pink dildo, I'm blushing.

He holds it up. "Can I use this on you?"

My arousal comes roaring back.

Marco props my hips up with a pillow this time, and then slowly pushes the toy inside of me. It's embarrassing at first, how hard he's staring at it when I glance at him over my shoulder, but then I forget to be embarrassed as he fucks me hard with the toy.

I come screaming.

I'm barely conscious when Marco cleans me up with a warm wet washcloth. He makes me get up to pee, and when I come back, he's changing the sheets. Marco tucks me in, tells me to take a nap, and the last thing I remember is a kiss on the forehead before I drift off to sleep.

23

MARCO

The morning of Christmas Eve, I take the train out to Long Island and I visit my brother's grave.

Brin's babysitting today, which is good because we needed a break to hydrate and get some fresh air after our two-day sex bender. I've always loved being around Brin—she's light and funny and kind—and all of these traits blossom in the bedroom. I've never felt a connection like this with someone before. And the fact that she was willing to explore was fucking hot as hell.

I grew up in Smithtown, but my brother is buried closer to the city in a Catholic cemetery. Against his wishes.

I don't visit on the day of his death or on his birthday. Instead I visit on the day my parents kicked him out.

I'm an atheist. I don't believe in God or an afterlife. But on the off chance that I'm wrong, the only thing I care about is my brother knowing how much I loved him.

When I get to the grave, I'm surprised to find a small wreath on the headstone. I'm even more shocked that there's a rainbow ribbon woven through it. This is not a queer-friendly community and even though I don't know this particular church, I would be shocked if they allowed this here.

I spot a tag on the back of the wreath and carefully flip it over. My breath catches in my throat when I read the hand-written note.

Joe-
I saw this and thought of you. I always think of you around the holidays.
Stay merry & bright.
Love, Drew

Drew was my brother's best friend, the one we lived with for a while. Since Joe's death, we drifted apart.

I put the wreath back, and then sit down and talk to my brother. I tell him all about my life in the past year. About William, and Bea, and mostly Brin. I talk about Brin so much, if there is an afterlife my brother is looking down on me and saying, "Jesus, man, I get it, you love her."

On the trip back to Manhattan, I text Drew.

MARCO

> I went to Joe's grave today and saw the wreath you left. Thank you for doing that.

I get a text back immediately.

DREW

> MARCO OMG HI

> How are you?

> I think of you so much at Christmas time.
> And Joe, of course.

ME

> I think of him a lot too.

We text updates about our lives—Drew sends me a picture of him and his boyfriend and their dog—and then he invites me to his house for dinner tonight. I hesitate for a moment, but then Drew sends me three more texts.

DREW

Just bring yourself. It's totally casual.

Do you remember that year Joe went tinsel crazy? It was gold strands EVERYWHERE and we found them for months and months afterward.

I'm so glad you reached out. I hope there's a shiny thing in your life somewhere that's Joe's style.

That makes me smile, especially from his use of the word shiny. Not only does it make me think of the scavenger hunt, but it's the perfect word to describe Brin. I also think about the decorations up in William's penthouse. Joe would have loved them. Just like Brin did.

I text Drew back that I'll be there, and ask if I can bring a friend. He says yes. Then I gaze out the window of the train.

Since Joe's death, I hadn't wanted to decorate for Christmas, especially not with a tree. His death was too raw. But now, after this holiday scavenger hunt and Brin's unbridled enthusiasm, maybe I'm ready for some of it in my life again.

And I know where I can steal some Christmas magic.

24

BRIN

THE CHAIN IS ON OUR DOOR. THE CHAIN IS *NEVER* ON OUR DOOR. We live in a safe building with a nice little community feel—unlike some of my apartments in the past.

"Brin?" Marco's voice calls from inside. My stomach does a flip of excitement at hearing his voice after everything we've been through the past few days.

"Yeah, it's me," I reply. Marco was gone when I woke up this morning, and hadn't returned by the time I'd left for babysitting. I worried about him, going out to Long Island by himself. I hope it was cathartic for him.

But right now, I think all the sex in the past two days wore me out. And Noah was hyped up on Christmas excitement, and for someone who didn't work her regular job yesterday or today, I am exhausted.

"Hang on, I'll get the chain."

I close the door and Marco removes the security chain. Then the door swings open and . . .

"Oh. My. God."

Our apartment *sparkles*. I recognize the decorations as having come from Billy Bob's apartment, and I can't believe Marco took them. There's real evergreen boughs draped over the windows in the living room, and a wreath with ribbon and pearly strands sits on the coffee table AND OH MY GOD THERE'S A CHRISTMAS TREE.

It's a little one that comes up to my chin, but it is stuffed full of ornaments and sparkling lights.

"You did all this?"

Marco rubs the back of his neck. "Yeah. This was all going to waste at William's place and I thought maybe you'd like it."

"*Yeah* I like it. But I didn't think you wanted to decorate. What changed?" *Please don't tell me this is sympathy I'm-sorry-I-defiled-you decorations.*

Marco clears his throat and looks down. I immediately go to him and circle my arms around his waist. He tells me about finding the wreath and talking to Drew while I hold him tight. It's emotional for him, and I can hear how much it meant to him to have someone else honoring his brother in a way he would have wanted.

"I thought Drew was right, you know? My brother loved the holidays and I can reframe it to think about him in remembrance instead of loss."

I put my chin on his chest so I can look up at him. "I am so glad that you reconnected with Drew."

"Me too. Actually, he invited me to Christmas Eve dinner tonight. I was hoping you could come with me."

I mock gasp. "Who me? Attend a Christmas party?"

He rolls his eyes at my antics, but he's smiling.

"I was going to try to talk you into a Christmas movie tonight. But a party sounds way better."

"It's not a party," he warns. "Just dinner."

I'm so eager to meet Drew, this friend of Marco and Joe's from the Before Brin times, that all of my exhaustion from earlier is forgotten.

———

D REW AND HIS PARTNER, I OANN, LIVE IN A CHARMING AND WARM brownstone in Clinton Hill. Their Christmas tree sits in the window overlooking Lafayette and their dining room, while narrow, is cozy. Along with the hosts, there's also Megan, a tiny woman Ioann dances with at a ballet company, and Nevaeh, Ioann's fourteen-year-old from his first marriage. The six of us fit comfortably in the space dominated by dark wood wainscoting and a bricked-in fireplace. An elderly pittie snores in the dog bed close to the stairs, worn out from the excitement of having guests.

With such a small group, maybe Marco was right about this not being a party. But it's even better, because once we've finished eating, we linger around the table over wine and our empty plates.

The whole evening has been awash in laughter and old stories. Drew has so many fond memories of Joe, and I can see Marco drink them in like a parched well.

"Do you remember," Drew says, holding up his red wine, "our first Pride Parade?"

"Do you mean the Pickle Pride Parade?"

"And by pickles, you mean . . ." Ioann says with his thick Russian accent. Then he makes a rude gesture that has everyone laughing, and Drew tries to cover Nevaeh's eyes.

The teenager rolls their eyes. "I don't want to hear about weird sex things. Can I be excused?"

Without waiting for an answer they get up.

Drew shouts, "It's not a sex thing. We *smelled* like pickles. Don't you want to know why?"

Nevaeh takes an oversized Nirvana sweatshirt off one of the kitchen barstools and slinks upstairs.

"Well, I wanna know why you smelled like pickles," Megan tells Drew.

His eyes crinkle. Drew is in his thirties, dark hair and eyes like Marco but his skin is light brown. "We wanted to tie-dye clothes and read that vinegar would make it brighter. But all it did was make it smell bad."

"But we weren't gonna show up to Pride without some kinda rainbow," Marco adds.

"And Joe wanted to be *decked out*." Drew flips his hand for emphasis. "You should have seen his hippie-dippie pickle-smelling crop top."

"He got invited up onto the stage at one of the shows, I forget which one, and the whole time I could only think about those drag queens wondering what the fuck smelled like pickles."

Drew leans back, chuckling. "Joe could be a wild child sometimes. But his confidence came from knowing he had you to look out for him."

"I didn't do anything," Marco mutters.

Drew sits up, leaning in, and his voice firms. "You did. I know how much you saved Joe when you two came to the city. Marco is the hardest worker I know," Drew says, looking around the table. "He knew more about housing protections and reporting discrimination than anyone. He made sure all us young broke kids knew what our rights were."

Under the table, I put my hand on Marco's thigh and squeeze.

"You two had your parts. You took care of Joe, Joe made sure you had fun," Drew adds.

Marco huffs a laugh. "He was always taking us to drag shows and queer clubs."

"Exactly," Drew says. The conversation moves to other things: dancing, Ioann and Megan's upcoming duet for next year's ballet, raising a teenager, and Drew's work as a lobbyist.

Later, I'm admiring their Christmas tree with Megan while the men wash dishes. "They have a beautiful tree," Megan says. "I like the homemade decorations." Megan's been best friends with Ioann for years, and she's originally from California. She's not at all what I would have expected from a principal ballerina—down to earth, warm, but quiet.

I snort. "You should see the tree Marco brought me today." I tell her about Billy Bob's decorations while looking for the homemade ones on the tree in front of us. They're scattered throughout the "nicer" ornaments, glass globes in gold, blue, and silver.

The homemade ones, though, are picture frames, hand painted with ribbons and rhinestones. They're not Martha Stewart, but they're obviously made with love.

"Brin, isn't this Marco?"

Megan holds out an ornament. It's round and painted in bright candy stripes. Sure enough, there's Marco, his arm looped around the neck of a softer version of him.

I take the ornament and peer at it. "That's Joe," I whisper.

We bring the ornament over to the guys, and Drew smiles at it fondly. Marco dries his hands and carefully takes the ornament from me.

After a few minutes of reminiscing, with Marco telling us the story about the day the picture was taken, Drew says, "You should take that one."

"No, I couldn't," Marco protests.

"We have a tree to hang it up on now," I point out.

"I have the supplies to make more. And I still have that photo saved somewhere. I can make myself a new one," Drew insists.

Marco takes it, and when we get home, he hangs it up on our pint-sized tree, right by the top.

"It's the best ornament on the tree," I say.

Later, when Marco is showering and getting ready for bed, I text Drew. We'd exchanged numbers before we left his house, and the ornament we brought home gave me an idea.

I haven't gotten Marco anything for Christmas, since he didn't celebrate, but I'm going to get him a last-minute gift in case he gets a tree to decorate for next year.

25

BRIN

THE ONLY THING THAT WAKES ME UP FASTER THAN A HAND-delivered caffeinated beverage is the dawning realization that I've started my period.

"Shit," I say, rolling onto my back. Merry Christmas to me.

"Brin, you okay?" Marco calls from the living room. Our bedroom door is closed.

"Yeah, I'm fine." Last night after the party we'd crossed another item off our sex to-do list: shower sex. Or, really, it was more Marco watching me with the showerhead, which was wildly hot. My cheeks heat just thinking about it.

I sling an arm over my eyes, attempting to pull myself together enough to check to see if I bled onto my sheets—Marco's sheets, at that. Doubly embarrassing.

I need to shower and—I sit bolt upright. "Fuck."

"Brin?" Marco's edge of concern in his voice has increased. "I'm coming in."

The door opens and Marco peers around the room before settling his gaze on me. His brows draw together. "What's wrong?"

I swing my legs over the side of the bed and quickly check

the fitted sheet behind me. Oh good, there's no stain. "I started my period."

"Oh." He relaxes in the doorway. "Merry Christmas?"

I snort. "The best part is that Bea took the rest of the tampons. In her defense, she texted me a reminder to pick some more up and I forgot." Of course Bea remembered to pack tampons for her trip. She probably uses one of those apps that tracks her cycle so she's always prepared.

As for me, I have attempted a few times to make notes in my phone's calendar about when my period starts, but whenever it hits I always think I'll make a note later, until I realize my period's over and I can't remember which day it started and I never made a note.

So yeah. Not very effective.

"Do you need me to run to the store?" Marco doesn't wait for an answer, but grabs his wallet from his nightstand.

"You don't mind?"

He shakes his head. "What else might you need?"

I tick off the other period supplies: Midol, panty liners, and a heating pad if it gets really bad. All present and accounted for, so I tell Marco what tampons to get and he heads out.

I shower and put in a liner when I get dressed, hoping it'll last till he gets back. I go to light my Christmas candle—it made it all the way to the day of Christmas!—but the lighter goes *click-click-click* and produces no flame.

Hmm.

I think I have another lighter in the closet, so I root around in there looking for it.

We've got one of these fabric shelf organizers hanging from the middle of the rod, designating a his side/her side approach to things. But as I'm digging through the stuff on my side, some of Marco's things fall out of the closet.

Two things, actually. Cranberry-red pillars that smell like Holiday Sparkle.

I hold them both up. They're about as equally burned down as the one on my nightstand.

Why does Marco have two more of my candles?

The front door opens and I push the candles back to roughly where they came from. I meet Marco at the door to our bedroom.

"Tampon delivery." He holds up the box.

"Thanks." I grab the box and retreat to the bathroom. When I come out, Marco's lounging on the couch.

"What do you normally do on period days?" he asks me.

I snort. "Pop some Midol and go to work."

"Okay, let me rephrase the question. What would you *like* to do on a period day when you don't have to go to work?"

I purse my lips, thinking. "Build a pillow fort, lie in it with a heating pad while eating ice cream and watching movies."

He rolls off the couch. "Let's do it."

———

FIFTEEN MINUTES LATER I'M RELAXING IN THE PILLOW FORT. THE heating pad is plugged in behind me, and even though the cramps haven't been too bad yet, it feels good.

Marco had told me he was going to make me a proper Christmas morning breakfast instead of ice cream. I'm not entirely sure what he considers a "proper Christmas morning breakfast." His usual breakfast is overnight oats, so I'm hesitant.

Also, based on our cookie baking adventure, I'm concerned about leaving Marco alone in the kitchen. The living room still smells like raw dough.

But it is being overpowered by the delicious aromas coming from the kitchen. Cinnamon and browning butter and sugar.

"What do you want on your French toast?" Marco yells.

This I have to see. I leave my warm cocoon and walk into

the kitchen just in time to witness Marco flip the last slice of bread in a pan. All four pieces are now brown side up, which explains the smells.

I fold my arms and lean my hip against the counter. "We had ingredients for French toast?"

"I bought them yesterday."

Yesterday, when Marco was letting the floodgates open on Christmas. There's a selection of toppings on the counter: whipped cream, maple syrup, strawberries, chocolate sauce. Basically anything to satisfy a sweet tooth craving, and he bought all this *before* I started my period.

Wait.

"Did you know I was going to start my period today?" It wouldn't surprise me. Marco's observant enough to notice signs, whether they are tampon wrappers in the trash can or two temperamental roommates.

Marco raises an eyebrow. "How would I have known that?"

I shrug. And then squint suspiciously at him. "So you happened to buy French toast supplies?"

Marco piles the slices on a plate. "I wanted to do something nice for you. After yesterday—I mean, we both worked really hard on the scavenger hunt, and this is a way to say thank you."

He hands me the plate and starts another batch. "Go ahead back to your pillow fort and pick a movie. I'll be there soon."

———

A couple hours later we've finished watching *How the Grinch Stole Christmas*—the animated version, not the Jim Carrey one—*A Charlie Brown Christmas*, and *Rudolph the Red-Nosed Reindeer*. Marco had joined me while I was still working through my pile of strawberry-and-whipped-cream-covered

French toast, and he hadn't said a peep about my movie choice. I've turned off the heating pad and have curled up on my side in the pillows.

Our plates are on the coffee table, which I pushed over to the side of the room under the window. The French toast was amazing, though Marco refused to match my sweet tooth bonanza and instead had poured an austere amount of maple syrup over his serving.

It's still a big improvement over his oats, so I'll take it as a win.

In the middle of *Rudolph*, my phone dings with a text message.

DREW

Operation Santa's Sleigh is complete.

BRIN

OMG you are the best!! Thank you thank you thank you!

I roll onto my side and bat my eyelashes at Marco. "Can you do me a favor?"

"Sure." He sits up. "Do you need your heating pad again?"

"No." I bite my lip, trying to stop smiling like an idiot. "There's a package down at the front. Can you get it for me?"

Marco's brows draw together. "Of course. Did you order something? You know I would have run out."

I make a shooing motion and Marco heads downstairs. When he comes back up, he's carrying what is clearly a wrapped basket, complete with bows and mistletoe. Drew really outdid himself.

"What is this?" Marco kicks the door closed.

"My Christmas gift to you," I say sweetly.

"Brin," he admonishes, but he sits down on the floor next

to me and sets the basket in front of him. "I didn't get you anything."

I gesture at the decorations from Billy Bob's. "I beg to differ. Also, don't act like you haven't been switching out my candle to make it last longer or fixing my Christmas lights." I sit up.

"How exactly did this happen, though?" Marco gestures at the over-the-top wrapping.

"I had help from Drew."

"Oh, that explains a lot." Marco shakes his head fondly. "He can be extra with the arts and crafts."

I smother my smile while Marco opens his present. Drew really is extra, because he's absolutely stuffed the basket with supplies. There are unpainted picture frames, paint, a storage caddy full of rhinestones, and even some funky tool to bedazzle things.

And there's an envelope stuffed with pictures of Joe. Marco thumbs through them, blinking back tears. Sometimes it's Joe by himself—I particularly like the one in front of the New York Public Library where Joe impersonates one of the lions—but more of them are with Marco or Drew.

"We have time," I say, "if you want to make some ornaments now. I have a couple hours before I leave for Eva's party. Although . . . are you sure you don't want to come with me?" I'd asked Marco weeks ago, and he'd declined the invitation. It's at Eva's parents' house, and it's a white elephant gift exchange with a bunch of her friends and family.

Marco hesitates, glancing at the picture in his hand. Joe's sitting on Santa's lap, blowing the camera a kiss.

"I'm sure Eva would be happy to have you," I wheedle.

"Eva or you?"

"Both, of course."

"All right, I'm in."

I clap my hands together. "Good. Let's make ornaments

and then we've got to run and get you a present though. Nothing too expensive, and the weirder the better. Come on!"

26

MARCO

Brin was not kidding about the white elephant gift needing to be weird. I was nervous sitting down around the tree with Eva's friends, knowing what I'd brought to the party.

Now that it's my turn, though, three gifts have been opened and two have already been stolen. Neither of them are the gifts Brin or I brought—there's a bag of miniature rubber ducks, a resin toilet seat with flowers encased in it, and a pack of Jane Fonda workout VHS tapes.

Eva's nineteen-year-old cousin hadn't known what they were, which made me feel every one of my thirty-two years.

That's what I'm choosing between, or one of the many presents that sit unopened under the tree.

I lean into Brin. "Do you have a particular attachment to any of the open ones?"

She bats her eyelashes at me. "'Cause you'd steal it for me?"

"Hell yes."

"Hmm." She taps her chin and looks thoughtfully at the pile. There are twenty of us here, so there's a lot to choose

155

from. Some of the gifts are fairly innocuous looking, like the two we brought, but some of them are wonky shapes.

Like the dick-and-balls-shaped one wrapped in green paper with a bow at the tip. Surely it's not actually a sex toy?

Well, there's only one way to find out.

Laughter fills the room when I grab the "penis" by the tip. Right away it feels vaguely familiar, but it barely weighs anything, so I doubt it's an actual dildo.

The whole room quiets while I open it. As I suspected, it's not a sex toy, but instead is an inflatable cylinder that says "Go Wildcats" and two poop-emoji stress balls. I wave the cylinder around and realize it's a thunder stick.

"A-plus for the packing effort," I say to the group.

"Thank you." Eva tosses her hair over her shoulder. I gently bonk her in the head with it.

Two turns later, someone steals from me and I have to go back to the drawing board.

Once I've made my choice and unwrapped a gently used game of Guess Who?, which the gift bringer modified to have pictures of *KPop Demon Hunters* characters instead of the normal people, Brin hops up from her spot next to me to use the bathroom.

Eva sidles in to take her place. When we walked into her apartment holding hands, Eva didn't bat an eye, just started introducing us around. Even now she doesn't have to say anything, she just looks at me smugly.

"You're not surprised," I say.

"No." She takes a sip of her chocolate mint martini. "I knew the first time you came to the bar late at night to walk her home that you two were gonna end up together."

That must have been ages ago. I don't even remember the first time I walked home with her. It doesn't happen all that often—only when I'm out late enough either with Greg or with William.

"She could use a guy like you. Someone to protect her. I hope she never loses that spark of innocence."

I'm not sure if Eva knew about Brin being a virgin, but she fixes me with a firm look. "If I have to protect her from you, I'm going to take every single aspect of your life down and you'll be forced to flee my city, do you understand?" Eva's glaring at me now.

I swallow, fifty percent glad that Brin has someone else who will watch her back, and fifty percent terrified.

"I understand."

"Good." Eva leans back on the couch and we watch someone pick up my gift and unwrap it—a book titled *The Fart that Changed the World*.

Eva cackles, and Brin returns from the bathroom to push her aside and sit between us. "Oh good, your gift was opened."

Brin goes a few turns later and steals the flower toilet seat. Someone steals that and then she unwraps a life-sized ceramic hissing duck.

We stay at the party long after the gift exchange is over. The food is good, the group is loud, and I've never seen Brin laugh so much.

It's no longer Christmas when we leave the party, hugging Eva goodbye. She makes sure we leave with our gifts—a box of penis pasta for me and the miniature rubber ducks for Brin —which both fit in a wine gift bag.

I wrap an arm around Brin as we walk toward the subway.

She leans her head on my chest. "Thanks for coming with me."

I kiss the top of her head.

"I wouldn't have had as much fun if I had to think about you being home alone."

"This was definitely better than being home alone." I

pause for a moment. "Actually, I think this is the best Christmas I've ever had."

Brin stops in her tracks and looks up at me. She's tipsy and tired, swaying on her feet. But her eyes are clear when she reaches up on her tiptoes and kisses me.

I don't let the kiss get too deep—we are standing on the sidewalk, people passing us occasionally and everything tinged in red from the stoplight at the corner.

"Come on," I say when I pull back. "Let's get home."

We ride the subway back to our stop and are home a few minutes later. We take turns in the bathroom, and when Brin slips back into the room, I hold my covers up. She smiles and slips in, reaching to turn out the light before I pull her back into my arms. How many nights will it take of Brin sleeping in bed with me before we get rid of the futon? With her soft body next to me, I want it to be now.

"How are you feeling?" I ask instead.

She hums and turns slightly toward me. "I took some Midol after my shower."

"Cramps?" I ask, lowering my hand to her belly.

"Lower back pain."

I push her, turning her gently away. She lies on her stomach and turns her head toward me. I kiss her shoulder and run my palm down her back to where her cotton shirt meets her pajama pants and dip my hand underneath to the small of her back.

She hums in pleasure when I knead first one side and then the other with my thumb. All it takes is a few minutes and Brin's breathing evens out, deepening.

Leaving me in the dark, wondering how I could have fallen so hard for my roommate.

27

BRIN

 restaurant for my shift. I'm working the lunch shift on our first day open after the holidays, so I had to get up with a (relatively) early alarm. I woke up alone in Marco's bed, him clearly having left for a run already. He wasn't back by the time I rushed out the door, so I haven't seen him yet today.

I flush and Eva laughs. She draws closer so as to not be overheard while we walk back to the employee locker room. "We barely had a moment by ourselves at the party. I have to know; tell me everything about you and Marco!"

I instantly blush.

Eva's jaw drops open. "Did you two have sex?"

"Shhh! Oh my god, Eva."

She laughs. I take a minute to shove my purse in the locker as I tell Eva the basics of how it went down. Actually, I tell her a lot about the scavenger hunt we did, and all of the sweet moments leading up to getting into bed together.

And then I tell her about starting my period yesterday.

Eva fans herself. "The only thing sexier than a man who gives you plenty of orgasms is a man who pampers his woman."

We finish in the locker room and head out for the pre-shift meeting, but Eva's words sit in my head all day. Marco takes care of the important people in his life, whether it's his boss or his brother, and I have no doubt that he would treat me carefully.

After the lunch rush, Eva nudges me toward the bar. I look over and there Marco is, drinking a Diet Coke and scrolling on his phone.

"Hi," I say. This time, instead of saying hello across the bar, I've come up behind him.

"Hey." He turns, spinning on the barstool, and glances around before leaning in. "Am I allowed to kiss you at your job?"

"Please," I say, and he stands to cup my face and press a kiss to my lips. "I'm almost done," I say when he pulls back.

"I'll be here," he says.

Fifteen minutes later, we're walking hand in hand back to our apartment. "Have you heard from Bea?" Marco asks.

I shake my head. "Not in a few days. I think she's coming home tonight, though, right?"

"I think so too." While we wait at a crosswalk, Marco pulls me in for a kiss. "How do you feel?"

"Fine. My feet and lower back are tired."

"You know, I've heard that orgasms are good for period pain." He raises an eyebrow.

The light changes and we step off the curb, Marco using our entwined hands to navigate us through the foot traffic. I like when he steers us like this. "How would that work, exactly?"

"What do you mean?" He studies me now that we're on the sidewalk and in the flow of traffic again.

"How would you want to . . . do that? I mean, with like . . ." My face is overheating.

"I think what you're asking me is how far I'm willing to go while you're bleeding, right?"

"Yeah."

Marco pulls me to the side, against a Christmas-themed shop display. Reindeer antlers seem to sprout from Marco's head as he looks down at me. "I would do anything you wanted." I start to protest, and he looks at me sternly. "Anything. Fingers, mouth, my dick. Whatever you want."

"Mouth?" I echo.

Marco stares at me. "Is that a request for that particular act or a clarification?"

I shake my head. "Neither. I'm reminding myself that you're a lot more experienced than I am and if you say you'd do that, then you'd do it."

One side of his mouth tips up and he leans in even closer. "I definitely want to eat your pussy again when you're ready."

My eyelids involuntarily flutter and suddenly our hips are a lot closer than they were before. Marco moves our tangled hands behind my back to pull me closer and he kisses me hard, right there on the street.

When he pulls back, I'm breathing hard. "I want . . . I mean, that sounds like a bit much. But someday, yeah. I'd like that." I swallow as Marco hums in excitement. "My period is usually heavy the first two days, so maybe you can use your fingers on the outside?"

Marco takes his free hand and cups between my legs. No one can see what he's doing except for maybe the reindeer in the window. "Play with your clit?" He says it low and gravelly.

"Yes."

"Fuck," Marco says. "All right, let's go."

28

BRIN

"Do you want the heating pad?" Marco asks when we get home. Our living room is still covered with pillows and blankets from my pillow fort, and the heating pad is down there too.

My lower back does ache, so I say yes, but first I go to the bathroom and pop another Midol. Then I change clothes and when I come out of our room, Marco's on the floor waiting for me. He's staring at the Christmas tree in the corner. "You know, I think it looks better here than at William's," he says.

"I agree." I flop down next to him. The heating pad's already on, and I wiggle into place. Marco props himself up on an elbow and gently rubs his thumb over my stomach.

"Comfy?"

"Yeah."

"Good." Then he leans in to kiss me. It's slow and tender, and when I roll toward him, looking for more, he pushes me back down and settles himself on top of me, between my thighs.

We keep kissing, slow and languid. Marco keeps it that way; anytime I try to push for more, he slows down again until it feels glacial. Drugging.

I finally reach down and pull at the back of Marco's shirt, lifting it up and over his head. This opens a whole new world for my hands to roam, skin on skin. I get so distracted, Marco breaks our kiss and starts making his way down my neck.

Under my hands, Marco's back is hot and firm. His muscles under my left hand, the ones that are preventing him from squishing me, are tight, flexed. The other side moves, the shoulder blades under my hand shifting as Marco runs his palm to my ribs.

His mouth moves gently over my neck, the soft skin meeting and sending shivers down my spine. I'm wearing a spaghetti-strap tank top, and Marco nudges the strap with his nose, trailing kisses down my collar bone.

"Why are you going so slow?" I pant out. "I'm not a virgin anymore." My voice is whiny, needy.

I can feel his smile. "No. I'm going this slow because I want to taste every inch of you."

I groan and Marco chuckles into my skin. He takes ages exploring across my collar bone, my sternum, and then finally the neckline of my top falls low enough to expose a nipple to his hot mouth.

"My god." When he sucks on it, my whole body bows. My hands fly to his head, where I can grip his hair in my fingers and keep him right where I want him.

The more he winds me up, the more I feel my body clamping down—my thighs are tight against his torso, enough that I feel like my thighs might have bruises tomorrow.

"Can you touch me? Please."

Marco lifts his head, smiling, and presses a kiss to the top of my breast. He drags a hand to the waistband of my boxers, hooking both the shorts and my underwear with a finger, but I still it.

"Maybe leave the underwear on?"

He looks up at me. "Of course." And then he's pushing

the boxers down, I'm kicking them off, and his palm is between my legs, the heel of his hand hitting *just so* and the pressure is glorious.

He goes back to lavishing my breasts with attention and it's like a string pulling tight from the crown of my head to the tip of my toes. Marco keeps the pressure steady and circles, circles over and over again until I break with a whimper and gasp, my body bowing up. He kisses my forehead as my whole body pulses.

When I finally relax, he follows me down. "God you're beautiful," he says.

My eyelids flutter and I hum in pleasure, contentedness filling an ache I've been carrying around for longer than I realized. Being with Marco, under his care, was better than I could have expected.

We lie still for a few moments, Marco lazily touching me. When I feel like I've caught my breath, I turn to him. "Is it— nope. Wait. Can I touch you now?"

Instead of answering, Marco rolls to his back. He shoves his pants down and off and holds the base of his dick so it angles straight up. It's hard and tight, the head already leaking with precum.

I squirm down to be level with it and suck it into my mouth.

"Fuck!" Marco shouts. He pushes me to get off and I sit up.

"What? I thought it was okay!"

"It is, it is. Ha. You caught me by surprise and I'm really on the edge." He's doing a half-laugh, half-groan, which I take as a good sign.

I open my mouth to take him in more gently, but we both freeze. There are voices right outside the door, and then a jangle of keys . . .

Marco and I both move at the same time, running for our bedroom.

29

MARCO

BRIN AND I CAREEN INTO THE BEDROOM AND I SLAM THE DOOR behind us. I'm completely naked and Brin's in her underwear.

Bea's voice comes from beyond the door. "Everyone okay in there?"

"Yup, just fine," Brin answers, her voice at that high-pitched level when she's stressed. She throws on a shirt—one that happens to be mine. I pull on a pair of pants.

"We don't have to go out there, do we?" Brin hisses.

"I don't think so." If we do, I'm very aware that I have a boner, and it's bad enough that we didn't, I don't know, leave a sock on the door or something. I run my hands through my hair and tense my thigh muscles, trying to get it to go down.

Brin drops down to sit next to me. "This is so embarrassing. Are we going to stay in here? What if they don't leave?"

As if she heard us, Bea knocks on our door. "We're dropping my stuff off," Bea says through the closed door. "We'll just be a few minutes and then I'm going to Charlie's."

I look up and call out. "You don't have to go, Bea."

"I want to. I'll text you, but I'll be back tomorrow." There's

167

a male voice, muffled, and then Bea says, "Or maybe in a few days."

She moves away from the door, and Brin flops back onto my bed. We listen to Bea and the man—Charlie?—move around the apartment.

Brin rolls onto her side to look at me. "I wish I knew Bea better. We text occasionally but she's so busy." She props herself up on an elbow to look down at me. "Did you ever want to be an executive assistant instead of a personal assistant?"

"I tried that once before," I admit. "I was the EA to a group of B-level managers at a tech company for a while."

"What happened?" Brin asks.

"I got fired."

"Let me guess: for being an asshole? Is that what you're going to tell me?"

I reach a hand out to Brin's hip and squeeze. "I was an asshole," I say. "But honestly, those guys I worked for were worse. All men, and some of the shit they wanted me to do . . ." I shake my head. "I got fed up with it. It was 'fudge a line here' and 'backdate this' to help their bottom line, and that was just my first few months. They eventually were charged with fraud by the SEC."

Brin watches me for a moment, eyes flickering back and forth between mine. "What do you like about your job now?"

"This is starting to sound like a therapy session," I joke.

Brin chuckles. Outside our door, Bea's and Charlie's footsteps pass and the apartment door closes as they leave. "But we're roommates and . . . lovers?"

"You're my girlfriend," I say firmly.

Her face heats, but she smiles. "And you're my boyfriend. If there's anyone you're going to talk to about these things, shouldn't it be me? I mean, yes, by all means, get a therapist, too. But I want a relationship when I can tell you everything."

I blow a breath out and close my eyes, leaning my forehead against Brin's chest. "You're right. Okay. What do I like about my job?" I think for a minute. "I'm never bored. Every day is different. My schedule is pretty great—when William's out of town, like now, I have time off. I have autonomy that I wouldn't have anywhere else because when things need to be done William honestly doesn't care how it gets done. I like that it's my responsibility to execute. William tells me what he wants and I make it happen. And I'm good at it. I'm organized."

"You are. Does he ever ask you to do something you don't want to do?" Her fingers are stroking through my hair now, a soothing scrape against my scalp.

"Yeah, I don't *want* to do most of the things he has me do."

"But you've worked for Billy Bob for a while now. Clearly it isn't as bad as the EA job, right?"

"No, it's not." That makes me think, and Brin keeps stroking while I do. "William is shallow, spoiled, flighty, and obsessively picky, but he also has high standards and the means to make it happen. People aren't used to him, but I am. And he never has asked me to do anything immoral or illegal, unlike the tech bros."

"Some people might mistake what you do for being an asshole, but I don't. I see a man with a high moral compass, someone who wants to follow rules and meet expectations. So what if Billy Bob wants powdered sugar on his crème brûlée."

I groan and laugh against her chest. "Cocoa powder on his eggnog."

"Whatever," Brin continues. "He's allowed to have his preferences. He's allowed to have who he wants at his party." Brin puts her hands on my jaw and lifts my face up to hers. "What were you and Joe arguing about when he called you an asshole?"

The sting of thinking about it makes my whole body tighten. "We found our landlord in our apartment. No notice or anything, just used his master key and walked right in. We didn't know what he was doing in there. I wanted to hire a lawyer. But Joe's best friend, who we were living with, wanted to stay in the apartment and 'have a talk' with him. Joe was stuck between the two of us and had just been laid off from his job."

"Aw, honey." Brin looks at me with such tenderness. "Joe was in a hard place. It wasn't really about you." She touches her nose to mine and I wrap my arms around her. "Marco. You are enough."

30

MARCO

We lie on the couch, cuddling and talking until she has to go to work. I think about Brin's words. Part of my brain keeps thinking, "Yeah but she doesn't know . . ." as if looking for excuses not to believe her.

I accidentally drift off waiting for her to get home, and when I get up to run the next morning, Brin is rock-solid asleep.

When I'm back from my run, she's at brunch with Bea. The minute I hear her key in the door I'm on my feet.

Brin leaps at me and I catch her, mouth already bearing down on hers.

"Bea's not with you?" I ask between kisses.

"She's at Charlie's," Brin explains, pulling my T-shirt over my head. "All weekend."

I groan and walk backward to the couch. "What time do you have to go to work?" When my knees hit the edge, I sit, Brin in my lap. She quickly wriggles off. "What are you—"

Brin tugs at my waistband, making her intentions clear. As soon as my dick is free, she licks the length of it.

She pauses to look up at me. "I have to leave in twenty minutes." And then she sucks me as far down as she can.

My fists are balled at my side and I'm using every ounce of restraint to not grab her. I don't even know what I would do if I did—I just know that I simultaneously want this and a million other things at the same time.

Brin hums, one hand holding my dick straight up while she licks and sucks the top. "I like doing this," she says.

"It feels really good," I tell her, panting. She works me over, teasing and tasting until I'm vibrating with tension.

She smiles and presses a kiss to the tip. "Put your hands behind your head?"

"Bossy." I do as requested. My sweatpants and boxer-briefs are around my ankles now.

Brin's eyes run over my chest and arms, gaze heating as she takes me in. I stretch and flex for her.

She retaliates by sucking me into her throat as deeply as she can again. I hiss and curve around her, but it's too late.

"Brin, I'm gonna come," I warn her.

She backs off enough to give herself breathing room and I blow, Brin swallowing as I pulse inside her mouth. "Okay, okay." I pull away when I get too sensitive.

Brin sits back. On her heels, looking smug and the most confident I've seen her. Soon, I hope to put that look on her face any time we're intimate.

"Okay, I've got to go to work," she says, popping up from the floor.

"Wait, wait. I want to make you come. I can be quick."

"Tempting," she teases. "But I don't want to rush."

"Yeah that's fair." I pull my sweatpants up and follow her into the bathroom. She starts brushing her teeth, and I lean against the door. "Sorry you can't make it to the party tonight," I say.

By our calculation, we earned thirty-nine points for the activities we completed. We won't know the judges' points we're awarded until tonight, so I promised Brin I'd text her as soon as I find out at the party.

She offered to try to switch her shift with someone, but I told her not to worry about it. She already took a night off because I'd run her ragged with the scavenger hunt, and I don't want her to lose out on another shift.

Plus, I'd rather that she take time off for just the two of us to spend together. I don't want to share her with a room full of strangers.

Brin can't answer, 'cause she's brushing the taste of my cum out of her mouth, but I watch her for the pleasure of it. When our eyes meet in the bathroom mirror, hers crinkle.

Her toothbrush finally finishes buzzing and she spits in the sink. "Stop making me laugh."

I hold my hands up in mock offense. "I was just watching you. What's so funny about that?"

"I don't know! It's domestic."

I come up behind her. "We've been roommates for a long time." I kiss her shoulder. "I know you're my girlfriend now, but since we already live together this is off into the deep end."

"I know," she says, leaning her head back onto my chest. "I like it."

———

THE BALLROOM IS STILL DRESSED IN ITS CHRISTMAS FINERY, BUT now instead of a stage there's a DJ and a dance floor. Two bars are on either side of the room and I've got four drink tickets in my pocket—two for me and two for Brin.

To the right of the DJ is a scoreboard. The bottom twenty-seven teams are listed in order of their combined score. I quickly skim down until I find our names and run my finger across. Just like we thought, thirty-nine points for the activities, plus another eight for the creativity. That's forty-seven total points.

Damn. I was hoping for at least fifty, but we've fallen short. We're still in the top half, though.

I scan the list again, looking for Greg and his partner. They're not far above us in ninth place, with fifty-five points, so that means I've lost the bet.

The top three slots on the scoreboard are empty, waiting for the ceremony that will announce the winners.

I get in line at the bar and text Brin our results. I also tell her we lost to Greg but we're still in the top half of the scoreboard, to give her some context.

While looking for Greg, I notice that the projector screen next to the DJ stand is playing a slideshow of photos and videos from the teams. I watch with amazement. One team built a sleigh out of snow in the one hour that they had and posed with one of them as a reindeer. Next is a video with two guys holding stained-glass cookies up to the camera before tapping the cookies together in a toast and taking a bite. The "glass"—I can't begin to guess how they did it—shatters and makes a mess, leaving both of them laughing.

There's a gasp from the crowd around me when the next photo reveals a giant paper snowflake. This is one of the tasks we didn't complete, and there's no way we could have competed with the size of this thing—the photo is taken from above, and the snowflake is laid out on a gym floor, the team members lying on the ground next to it, arms and legs spread like they're trying to make snow angels.

By the time I get up to the bar to order a beer I've seen two of our submissions: our Christmas tree made from candy—it looks even brighter green on the big screen and we had to make the trunk *enormous* so it wouldn't collapse—and our sunny snow person.

"Marco!" A voice calls for me to my left, and I spot Greg and Luis at a high-top table. We shake hands and back-slap and Greg grins at me. "Did you see the scoreboard?"

I lift my beer to him. "Great job, you win."

"I can't wait to have my own assistant for a week." He rubs his hands together. "I might unleash you on my spreadsheet. I know you're an expert there."

"Don't threaten me with a good time."

We chat about the scavenger hunt and Greg and Luis tell me some entertaining stories about their adventures around the city. Soon, the lights are dimming and the music fades away.

"Welcome, SHiNY teams!" It's the same woman who kicked the scavenger hunt off.

We applaud, there's a welcoming speech, another speech by a guy on the board of one of the organizing charities, two more speeches, an award given to one of the corporate sponsors, and then they start announcing the top three teams, starting with the third place team. The announcer slips through the photos and videos the team submitted and they are amazing. The team with the giant paper snowflake is in third place and the second-place team had dressed up as Victorians to go caroling.

"And now, our winning team." Behind her, the screen is black. "We'd like to spotlight how far this team, with an astounding thirty-eight creativity points from the judges, went to come in first place."

The screen fades in and "Carol of the Bells" plays over the sound system. The video itself is in slow motion: snowflakes falling, walking through the woods, an axe striking wood.

It's a goddamn music video for chopping down their own Christmas tree. It's professional grade, and someone on that team has got to be a professional—or they hired one.

When the video's done, the room is filled with applause. Another video starts playing, but without sound now. It's as cinematic as the previous one. "With their thirty-eight judges' points added to the activity points, our winners of SHiNY, with a total of eighty-five points, are Jacob Templeman and Rebecca Foley!"

Everyone applauds as the team gets on stage and is handed their trophies and one of those giant fake checks.

"Oh shit, I know her," Greg says. "She's on Instagram and does these really popular underground concert pop-ups. No wonder she won."

"That explains the amazing videos," I add.

Once the applause dies down, the host steps back to the mic. "And our last award of the night goes to the team that raised the most money. As you know, this depends on both the team accumulating points *and* collecting pledges. The winner this year is Marco Russo and Brinda Shaw!"

Surprised that they would give out an award for that, I make my way through the crowd to collect our trophies. I shake hands with the people on stage and then go back to my table with Greg and Luis.

They congratulate me with handshakes and claps on the back. It feels disingenuous, since we only had one person pledge money for our team. Like maybe William should be here instead of me. Or at the very least, he should have gotten a trophy.

The music starts up again. As I chat with Greg and Luis, I debate about going home, but Brin's not home, so I might as well hang out with my friends.

Luis is telling me about a trip he took to Costa Rica when Greg nudges me. He lifts his chin to the screen and I look up to see myself skating toward Brin, stopping next to her so we can smile and wave at the camera and she can take a few tottering steps.

"So what's it like living with her?" Greg asks.

I blink at him. "It's great."

"I was wondering if you were roommates when I met her."

"When did you meet her?"

"Maybe eight months ago."

Yes, Brin had been living with me. I try to remember if Brin had ever said anything about a date, but if she did I can't remember.

Greg leans in and tilts his head toward Luis. "I told him all about Brin. So, like, does she bring the guys home with her?"

I take a sip of my beer, buying some time. I don't know what he's talking about, but I've often found that if you leave room in the conversation, people will tell you more. I tell the truth. "No, she doesn't."

Greg smirks. "I guess that would destroy the illusion, right? Those girls aren't there to bring men like us back to their shitty apartments."

"My apartment's not shitty."

Greg gives me a look. "I've been there. You definitely live below your pay grade. And you told me it was because your roommate couldn't afford better." He laughs. "She probably regrets getting off the app. If she was still there, she'd definitely be able to afford better."

"She is hot enough," Luis agrees.

"Are you still on the app?" I ask.

"Nah," Greg says. "They instituted an ID verification a while ago and I didn't feel like going through the effort. And it got to be like, what's the point? The women on Sugary were hotter and looking for guys to fuck, but it was too much work. They're all gold diggers, anyway."

This whole time, Greg's smiling. It raises my hackles. Maybe it's because there's a vibe of "it's not my fault these women don't want me" or his use of gold digger as a slur, or maybe it's because he's specifically talking about Brin.

Greg and I meet up a couple times a month. We race each other on runs, play one-on-one on the court, and talk shit about our bosses. He never has trouble meeting someone at the bar to take home. He's good-looking, charming, and he has clout—his boss has climbed the ranks in the art scene in leaps and bounds since Greg started working for him.

How well do I really know Greg? What signs have I missed about his behavior?

Because no one is going to talk about my girlfriend like that.

31

———

BRIN

WHEN I GET HOME, MARCO IS SPRAWLED ON THE COUCH, scrolling on his phone. He'd sent me updates throughout the night, which I saw when I was on break. Even knowing that we won an award, I still squeal when I see the trophies on the coffee table.

"Oh my god, they're frickin' cute."

I pick one up and inspect it. It's got a plaque on it that has Marco's name on it, and the trophy itself is a hand holding a snowflake aloft. It's dramatic and extra, but I don't care.

And I guess we have Billy Bob to thank for it.

Marco sat up when I came in, and he's watching me with a smile on his face. "Hi," I say, and lean down to kiss him. It's intended to be quick but Marco smells good—freshly showered and minty breath too.

When we pull apart, he pats the couch beside me.

"I need to shower," I say. I'm gross from work and smell like food.

"Give me a minute," he says. "I want to ask you something."

I don't like the sound of that. "Okay . . ." I sit.

"I was talking to Greg at the party."

I straighten my back. "Oh?"

"He told me about the app, Sugary? I looked it up when I got home. Can you explain it to me?"

Oh my god. I can't even begin to imagine what Greg told Marco. Is Marco mad I didn't tell him before we had sex? I never even slept with anyone, though!

And of course, there's my mom's voice in my head, the words of the church. I think of the countless times my mom has excused men's behavior because a woman dressed a certain way. If she were here right now, she'd say I deserved it because I put myself on that app.

Heart pounding, I wipe my hands on my pants. I remember when Eva described it to me, the words she used. "It's a dating app. On paper it's 'luxury dating' but in reality, it's rich guys who are looking for a low-commitment relation-ship that's more specific."

"Specific how?"

"I only went on a few dates through the app. But Eva's been on there for a while and she's probably the person you want to talk to."

Marco puts his arm over the back of the couch, his hand landing on my shoulder. He squeezes me gently. "Eva can do whatever she wants, as long as she's a consenting adult. I want to know about you."

I take a deep breath. "It's unspoken that these men are looking for women to spoil. Sugar daddies, though the website is clear that those kinds of relationships are not allowed. Eva likes it because she gets taken out to fancy meals and one of her dates gifted her an expensive purse and she sold it, and another one gave her like two hundred dollars for cab fare home after their date. And she only sleeps with the guy if she actually wants to. But . . . it's men, you know? Some of these dates are bound to go badly."

Marco's mouth tightens. "Did you go out on a date with Greg?"

"Yes. I'm really sorry I didn't tell you before." My eyes sting. I should have told him when I saw Greg at the scavenger hunt.

My fists are curled in my lap, and Marco picks one of them up and brings it to his mouth, pressing a kiss on the back of my hand. "What did he do?"

I take a deep breath. "We had one date. I could tell he thought I was going to sleep with him that night, and then he was pissed that I didn't go home with him. It was nothing he said right then, but the way he looked at me. And then he messaged me."

Marco leans back and draws in a deep breath.

They're just words, some of them I even believe, on some level, even though I don't want to.

I stand up. "I want to show you those messages."

"Brin, wait." Marco catches my hand. "You know I believe you, right? I don't ever want to be friends with someone who made you uncomfortable."

"I know," I say. Marco lets me go and I dig my phone out of my purse. I have to redownload the app and reset my password. A pop-up comes up that says, "Your account was suspended due to four weeks of inactivity. Would you like to reinstate your account?"

I click yes, and I'm brought to the home screen of Sugary. I take a deep breath and click on my inbox.

32

MARCO

Brin navigates to her messages and then scrolls up, reading as she goes. She pales, and her eyes get watery. My stomach feels like lead.

Brin hands me the phone, and I read the messages from Greg. And they're bad.

Really bad.

Unhinged.

I can't believe that my friend would send anyone this shit.

It started out with *not even a kiss goodnight?* and *I guess you wanted an extra incentive.*

When Brin didn't respond, it escalated.

The only thing worse than a slut is a cocktease.

Quit whoring yourself on this app if you're not gonna suck a dick.

Brin's face is pale and her eyes are welling up. "Hey." I drop the phone and take her hands in mine. "It's okay, come here."

"Why would he say those things?" Her voice is small as I tuck her into my chest. "I didn't even *do* anything."

"I know you didn't. That's not what this is about."

I hold her close while she takes deep steadying breaths.

183

Inside, rage boils. I want to rip into something; I want to scream at Greg; I want to scorch the earth.

But this is not about me, so I take deep breaths and focus on Brin. I hold her for a few minutes until she pulls away.

"What can I do for you?" I ask.

She rubs her forehead. "I'm not sure. I'm tired and I smell like garlic and butter and I'd like to shower and go to bed."

"Totally valid. It is late. Let's talk in the morning about making a plan, okay?"

She nods and gets up to shower. Later, we both lie in my bed, neither of us sleeping, but at least I can hold her close.

———

IN THE MORNING, I SIT UP IN BED ON MY PHONE. I BARELY SLEPT last night, still shaken about Greg's behavior. While Brin sleeps, curled up on her side, I do some light cyber stalking, reading back through my texts with Greg, scrolling his Instagram.

It's disturbing how none of it raises red flags, but I know bad people are good at hiding things. Does Greg even see his actions as bad?

Brin's alarm goes off. She reaches out to shut it off, and rolls over. "Hey." She gives me sleepy, happy eyes as she stretches. "Did you run already?" she mumbles. Brin wriggles over until her head is resting in my lap. I let my hand rest on her head and gently stroke her wild red hair.

"No run today."

She hums a deep sigh. "Lazy."

"I know. Don't fall back asleep." I shake her and she groans. "I'll make you coffee."

"Yesssss."

Brin gets up and shuffles to the bathroom. She leaves the door open while she showers. "Brin, you want me to toast a bagel?" She's got a sleeve of them on the counter. I hear what sounds like a yes so I fix breakfast for her and have it ready when she comes out of the bathroom, a turban around her head.

She eats her breakfast and then sits back, sipping her coffee. Then she blows out a breath. "So. Greg."

"What do you want to do?"

"I don't know. It's been a while, I'm not sure I can even do anything." Her eyes are on her coffee. "What would you do?"

When I hesitate, she looks at me. "I know you think you're an asshole. But Greg is really, truly, a bad man. It . . . it helped me to tell you. To see you get angry. You're the only person that knows about those messages and I don't want to let him get away with saying those things to me—or anyone else."

I fold my arms and rub my hand over my mouth. "You could report him to Sugary—I bet they have an anti-harassment policy, and I'm sure you're not the only one he's done this to. But the repercussions would be pretty light. I don't think he's using the app anymore anyway."

"I want there to be repercussions," Brin says firmly.

"You could go to the police."

She shakes her head. "What would they do? It's just a few messages, albeit they're threatening and scary. But he's not stalking me and he doesn't have any other way to reach out to me. Although now that he knows we're roommates, he knows where I live. I don't want to wait to see if he does something else."

I feel a pang of guilt. Greg helped me move Brin in here, for fuck's sake. And now she's going to feel unsafe in her own home? Greg needs to know that he's fucked up, and I want to make sure he gets exactly what he deserves.

"Another option is to approach his boss," I say.

Brin's eyes widen. "Get him fired?"

"Yeah. He probably has a morality clause in his job, because people like William don't want someone who's so close to them behaving in a way that makes them look bad. This is a perfect example. Ishimoto is a public figure."

Her surprise turns to determination. "Yes. That's what I want to do. How do we do that?"

I explain what I want to do and why. A hint of a smile shows on Brin's lips for the first time since she got home last night, and she nods eagerly. "If you think it'll work, let's do it. I don't want to see him again, I just want him stopped."

I hold out a hand. "Open up Sugary and give me your phone. I'll screenshot everything and send it to myself."

Brin follows my instructions. I text myself the images and hand her phone back. I spend a few minutes crafting an email. The trickiest part of this is making sure Greg's boss sees it. If I emailed the contact I have for him, Greg would probably get the message first, and it's unlikely it would ever get to Ishimoto. I hit send, and then make the call on speakerphone.

William answers on the fifth ring. "What is it?"

I have *never* called William on vacation, not even in my early days of working for him, and I'm thankful for that because William is going to take this seriously.

"I've never asked you for a favor, but I'm asking you for one now and I want you to act on it today."

William is quiet for a beat. "Go on."

I explain the situation. "I've sent you an email so you can see for yourself. I want you to contact Ishimoto personally—*not through Greg*—and make sure they see what Greg's done. If they don't fire Greg, I want you to never buy another of Ishimoto's work again, and sell all the ones you own."

"Anything else?" William asks dryly.

"We'll see how Ishimoto responds."

William is quiet for a moment, but I can hear him moving in the background. I wait.

"I don't like sticking my noses in other people's business. Why should I?"

"Do it or find another assistant." Brin's eyes widen. I wasn't planning on making the threat, but it feels right. If William isn't willing to stick his neck out for me, why should I keep doing it for him?

William's quiet again, and I think I've shocked him. "My, my," he says. "You certainly have a taste for vengeance. Who's Brie to you?"

All the screenshots of the conversation show her name as Brie. "Her real name is Brin." I meet those sky-blue eyes with mine. "She's the best thing that ever happened to me."

———

BRIN'S LIPS PART IN SHOCK. SHE KEEPS HER EYES ON ME UNTIL I get off the phone with William and then she crawls into my lap and kisses me, her hands on either side of my face.

When she pulls back, I tell her the truth. "Brin, I love you."

She sucks in a breath. "You do? Even though I'm a hot mess?"

I pull back to really look at her. "Why do you think that?"

She laughs, self-depreciatingly. "This is my third job this year. I can't even remember to track my period. I don't feel like an adult, ever."

"You don't give yourself enough credit." I stroke her cheek with my thumb. "I don't see someone who is struggling. I see someone who's bright and funny and too kind for her own good. Someone who's spontaneous and willing to jump in to help anyone who needs it, like the mom upstairs or the roommate who suckers her into a multiday wild-goose chase around the city."

She looks away from me, the compliments hitting her hard. "There's something you don't know, though." She swallows, and I feel it under my palm. "I have a lot of credit card debt. Like, *a lot.*"

"How much?" I ask.

A tear leaks down her cheek when she tells me. It is a lot; what a burden for her to be carrying.

"It's bad, I know," she rushes out. "I didn't know what I was doing when I first moved here and my shopping snowballed. For a while it was fine, manageable. And then my first roommate in the city suggested I sublet to them. I thought that was what you were supposed to do. And then they stopped paying and I couldn't get them to move out, and I lost the security deposit because of them and the utilities weren't getting paid."

She's crying now, and I pull her into my arms.

"So I thought I'd learned my lesson, and the next place we were co-tenants. But my credit score had taken a hit and so I took out a loan and then I still got fucking left in the lurch by my roommates. When I couldn't cover the rent, I had to take out two more credit cards or get evicted. See?" she says through her tears. Her arm snakes out to point at herself. "Hot mess."

I let her cry on my chest for a moment and then pull her back to look up at me. "A credit score is just one number. It's not a pass/fail for life, okay?"

"Okay." She sniffs.

"I do feel like there's a power imbalance, though. I don't ever want you to feel uncomfortable here, or that you have to stay with me because you can't afford to live anywhere else."

"Why do you say that as if it won't last?"

Now it's my turn to look away. "You saw me with Ash. You know what I'm like at my job." I swallow. "It bleeds into my real life. Joe thought I was an asshole and someday you will too."

Brin touches my chin, making me meet her eyes again. "I've lived with you long enough, Marco. I know who you are. And so did your brother. He loved you so much."

I nudge her hand and kiss her palm.

"Today those qualities that you think make you an asshole made me feel protected. I wouldn't have known what to do about Greg without you. I'm also not in that place that I was when we first moved in together," she continues. "I mean, I still have a lot of debt, and I'm working on it. Someday, I'll have an emergency fund, for when I need to fly home or break the lease on an apartment. And I have friends now too. I'm not alone. For example . . ."

She pulls her phone out of her pocket and taps the screen a few times. It rings on speaker three times until a female voice picks up. "Hey!"

Brin smiles. "Hey, Eva! Marco's here too."

"Marco! Are you calling with good news? Did you win the scavenger hunt?"

I laugh. "No, not even close."

"I've got a question for you," Brin says. "If I had to move out of my apartment with Marco right now, could I come stay with you until I find a new place?"

Eva's tone sharpens. "What did he do? Marco, *what did you do?*"

"No, no, Eva," Brin rushes to get out. "Hypothetically. He's worried he's taking advantage of me."

Her voice softens. "Oh my god, of course! You can sleep on my pullout couch and we can walk to work together. We can make it a sleepover with the three of us. I have these new stick-on nails I want to try, and Shannon likes this expensive face mask and she lets me mooch off of her. Maybe I'd even kick Shannon out and you can be my permanent roommate."

We hear a muffled "hey!" in the background. "Just kidding," she says, which is followed by laughter. Eva's voice comes back on. "Do I need to go over to your place and kick Marco's ass until he stops being so worried about you?"

I answer before Brin can. "Today is not that day, Eva, but hang on to that thought."

Brin frowns at me but Eva laughs. "Don't forget, babe: you

are a kick-ass woman, and you aren't going to ever let someone take advantage of you again. Got that?"

"Got it," Brin agrees.

We thank her and hang up the phone.

"What now?" Brin asks.

"The only thing that changes," I say, "is that we keep loving each other."

"Epically."

"And often," I add.

"And maybe we get rid of my futon?"

I answer by pulling her face down to mine and kissing her hard. This was definitely the best Christmas anyone has ever had.

EPILOGUE

Brin

IF I THOUGHT I'D GET SPOILED OVER BILLY BOB'S VIEW FROM HIS penthouse, I was sorely mistaken.

"How can Billy Bob go from this"—I wave my arms out at the painfully blue Caribbean water and the infinity pool that meets it—"and then back to the busy, gray, noisy city? I don't understand."

"I know," Marco says, leaning onto the glass banister that separates this patio from the one slightly lower that contains the pool. We have a view of the pool's view of the island's view of the ocean. It's like a Russian nesting doll of vacation one-upmanship.

"If my family had a house like this, I'd live here. Between a Manhattan penthouse and this paradise, I'd choose St. Bart's, one hundred percent."

Marco grins at me. I can't believe that we are getting to stay here for three full days.

While Billy Bob is still the annoying, vapid narcissist he's always been, he has softened somewhat toward Marco. We were still both shocked when Billy Bob suggested that we use his family's airplane and vacation home for a Valentine's Day getaway.

Granted, it's actually March, because Valentine's Day is massively busy at the restaurant and I worked my ass off so that I could afford to take this time off.

I also think it's a good thing Billy Bob doesn't know that I call him that. I almost slipped the first time I met him.

Billy Bob did pass along the information about Greg to Ishimoto, who fired him. We haven't seen or heard from Greg since then. And Billy Bob insisted on meeting me, since I was at least somewhat "responsible" for Greg getting fired and a witness to Ash's firing.

I'd never met a billionaire before. It was underwhelming.

But here I am, on a romantic vacation with the love of my life.

The pool has a bunch of lounge chairs with rolled-up bright red beach towels perched on the cushions, and I can't wait to sit down and relax and read a book, for once in my life.

Marco finishes giving me the tour—he's been here twice before—and that includes meeting the chef who's going to cook for us. I change into my bathing suit and ask Marco to slather sunscreen on my back.

I hold out my arms. "I'm going to be covered in freckles by the end of the trip. No, by the end of the day."

"I'll lick each and every one of them," Marco growls.

I grab my book and wander through the house—which is unobjectionally beautiful because it's a mansion in the Caribbean but also kind of ugly because someone decided glass chandeliers and a black-and-white theme were the way to go—out to the pool.

It's fifteen minutes before Marco joins me—a suspiciously long amount of time. I'm not sure what exactly he's up to, but I got a big hint last week when I was putting our laundry away and found a small velvet box.

Now he's carrying a platter of fruit and two frozen cock-tails. At Marco's request, the chef had prepared snacks and an easy dinner for our first night, which means we are now by ourselves.

Even though I'm now ten months away from being debt-free, I still don't feel like an adult that can be trusted with a multimillion-dollar house. It comes with a golf cart, and that alone could be complete mayhem.

I'll let Marco drive.

He settles next to me on the lounge chair under the umbrella and we toast. The daiquiri is perfect—more fruity than sweet and ice cold, which feels great because it's eighty-five degrees out.

"When we left the city it was forty-two degrees," I marvel. Bea had texted us "Bon voyage" when our flight took off with a winter storm on its tail. Later, she sent a picture of the street outside Charlie's place covered with swirling snow.

It's pretty much their place now, since Bea spends more time there than at our place. And our place is officially going to become "ours" next month, when Bea moves out for good.

I read for a while, a romantasy I saw on TikTok ages ago and never got around to starting. Next to me, Marco relaxes so hard, he might be asleep.

Which is why I'm startled when out of nowhere he says, "You know what I'm thinking about?"

"Dragons raised from the dead and threesomes in front of a fireplace?"

"No, that's you."

"Oh. What then?"

He points to the edge of the balcony railing. "No one can see us here. William said there are only security cameras pointing away from the property. So I can fuck you there." He moves his arm to the hot tub. "And there. And there's a private-access beach with an outdoor shower and a removable showerhead, and I'm definitely fucking you down there."

I pull my sunglasses down the bridge of my nose and look at his tented shorts. "My, my, that's quite a hard-on you've got there for fucking all over Billy Bob's house," I tease. "Why wait until we're down there?" I pivot my legs off the lounge and climb onto his lap.

Marco grabs my hips. "There we go," he says approvingly. I kiss him, tasting the sun and the sweetness of our drink. We grind and make out for a few minutes until Marco reaches between us to make sure I'm wet enough. Then he pushes my bikini bottom to the side and plunges two fingers in.

I ride his hand as he works the fly of his shorts open and strokes himself. "Come on, gorgeous. I want to watch you come."

I lean back, resting my hands on his thighs and grinding down. Marco adds a third finger, thrusting hard and aggressively pressing on my G-spot, just like I like it. I cry out, embarrassingly loud enough to worry the boats will hear my orgasm echoing off the water, but I don't have time to worry because while I'm still coming, Marco plunges me down onto his dick.

From there it's rocking my hips and chasing pleasure for both of us. When Marco gets close, he flips me onto my back and pounds into me. We're not using condoms anymore and when Marco comes, I feel it deep and hot.

I lie limp when he sits back, both of us breathing hard. After a few moments he gets up, and the water runs in the half bath by the pool. Marco returns with a wet washcloth to clean us up.

I am sweaty and overheated. "I'm getting in the pool," I announce. Marco follows me. It's chilly and refreshing and divine. We float and play until we get hungry, and then pad inside on wet feet with towels wrapped around our middles.

When we finish eating, Marco takes our plates and puts

them in the sink. "I have a surprise for you," he says, leaning on the kitchen island. His wallet is nearby and he opens it, pulling out a single slip of paper about the size of the ones you find in fortune cookies. He holds it out to me.

LOOK UNDER SOMETHING HOLLOW FOR THE NEXT CLUE.

I gasp. "A scavenger hunt?"

He crosses his arms on his chest and leans back, grinning, but his finger taps his bicep in nervous anticipation. I know exactly what's at the end of this scavenger hunt.

And I'm going to say yes.

———

The End

Want one more sexy scene with Marco and Brin at next year's Christmas? Scan the QR code to sign up for my newsletter for an exclusive bonus chapter.

Please Review

Reviews are critical to all authors. You can leave a review for *Run, Run, Roommates* at your preferred retailer and at Goodreads and BookBub.

For a list of Liz Alden's books, please visit lizalden.com/books

ACKNOWLEDGMENTS

I loved coming up with a charity scavenger hunt structure, but the idea itself came from Elia Winters, who participated in a real-life (though much more complicated) scavenger hunt called Great International Scavenger Hunt (GISH).

Greg's side plot was inspired by "Devil in Disguise" by Marino. The song went viral in the Formula One corners of the social internet and I couldn't get it out of my head. It's catchy, of course, but mostly I thought about how a man stealing your purse is the tip of the iceberg. There are so many other things we fear, worse things, that women (especially women of color) and queer folx have to face every day.

As this series has grown, so have I. And at a point in the world when there's so much to be angry about, I remind myself through my writing to keep up the fight, be more giving, more accepting, and, frankly, more gay.

I would not have gotten this book written without Felicia Daven, who I met with once or twice a week at our amazing local library to work on our stories. Shout-out to libraries and librarians!

Thank you to my early readers, Lainey Davis, Ember Leigh, Serena Bell, and Karen White. Your comments and feedback were tough but helped me write a better story.

Thank you to my proofreader, Dan Janeck, and to Qamber for the cutest covers for this series.

And as always, a big thank-you to my husband, who encouraged me so much from day one, and my parents, all five of them, who supported this book in one way or another.

ABOUT LIZ ALDEN

Liz Alden used to live on a sailboat with her husband. Now she's in her small town era and living in Western Mass.

She knows exactly how big the world is—having sailed around it—and exactly how small it is, having bumped into friends worldwide.

She's been a dishwasher, an engineer, a CEO, and occasionally gets paid to write or sail.

The books are inspired by her real-life travel.

Follow Liz:

www.ingramcontent.com/pod-product-compliance
Lightning Source LLC
Chambersburg PA
CBHW032222190726
48289CB00007BA/2346